PULP
Literature

Pulp Literature Press
Issue No. 43, Summer 2024

Publisher: Pulp Literature Press; Editor-in-Chief: Jennifer Landels; Senior Editor: Mel Anastasiou; Acquisitions Editor: Genevieve Wynand; Poetry Editors: Daniel Cowper & Emily Osborne; Assistant Editors: Sierra Louie, Ellen Spacey; Copy Editor: Amanda Bidnall; Proofreader: Sierra Louie; Graphic Design: Amanda Bidnall & Sierra Louie; Cover Design: Kate Landels; Subscriptions: Carol McCauley; First Readers: Amber Allen, Mark Cameron, Michaela Chan, Summer Keown, Sylvia Leong, Tara Smalldon. For advertising rates, direct inquiries to info@pulpliterature.com.

Cover painting, *Yellow Moon* by Joyce Harumi Kamikura. Illustrations for 'Fasteners' by Michaela Chan. All other illustrations by Mel Anastasiou.

Pulp Literature: ISSN 2292-2164 (Print), ISSN 2292-2172 (Digital), Issue No. 43, Summer 2024.

Published quarterly by Pulp Literature Press, 21955 16 Ave, Langley, BC, Canada V2Z 1K5, pulpliterature.com, at $18.00 per copy. Annual subscription $60.00 in Canada, $80.00 in continental USA, $92.00 elsewhere. Printed in Surrey, BC, Canada, by Fraser Printers Ltd. Copyright © 2024 Pulp Literature Press. All stories and works of art copyright © 2024 their authors as per bylines.

Pulp Literature Press is based in the unceded traditional Coast Salish Territories of the Katzie, Kwantlen, Matsqui, and Semiahmoo First Nations.

Pulp Literature Press gratefully acknowledges the support of the Canada Council for the Arts and the Government of Canada.

Pulp Literature is a proud member of the Magazine Association of BC and Magazines Canada.

TABLE OF CONTENTS

FROM THE PULP LIT PULPIT

Between Life and Dreaming

I love a great quote. Anna Quindlen, in *How Reading Changed My Life*, says, "Books are the plane, and the train, and the road. They are the destination, and the journey. They are home."

Books as both destination and journey resonate with my own readerly life, especially that of my younger years, when my freedom of exploration was limited to where my feet, the city bus, or my parent's yellow station wagon could take me. Books took me farther away than any of them. Even on actual trips into the actual world, I could usually be found curled up somewhere — including the back seat of that station wagon — reading. Those books introduced me to places, spaces, people, and times I could scarcely have dreamed of, even with life happening right there, on the other side of the page.

How has reading changed *your* life? I would imagine that for many of us, reading has made our worlds just a little bit bigger, and, perhaps, brought each of us just a little bit closer. And now summer is here and more storied adventures await, ready to be found via tickets to places near and far, or in stacks of books whose time has finally come. And wherever we go or however we get there, our fellow travellers will be right there with us, on the plane, and the train, and the road. We'll find them in the pages of our great summer read. Perhaps you will find a new companion right here, in these pages.

And when, after days or weeks or months away, we at last cross the threshold of our home's doorway, drop our suitcases, and breathe in the unfamiliar-familiar scent of home — or when we turn the final page of a favourite book — we feel, perhaps, a little relief. And a little sadness too. You can go home again. And half the fun is figuring out where you will go next.

~Genevieve Wynand

In THIS ISSUE

A magical *Yellow Moon* by **Joyce Harumi Kamikura** shines on our stunning summer cover, while feature author **Matthew Hughes** brings ancient gods to modern Italy in 'Forest of Shadows'. Women of all ages rise to adventure in 'Grandma Had Guns' by **Finnian Burnett**, 'Yakety Hex' by **KT Wagner**, 'Managing a Difficult Situation with Grace' by **Leslie Wibberley**, and 'The Golden Mare' by **JM Landels**.

Megan W Shaw in 'All but Pink', **Alan Sincic** in 'The Scientific

Method', and **Jodi MacAulay** in 'Girl of My Dreams' serve up varied ingredients for a life well lived. But time slips quickly by in the poetry of **Casey Killingsworth, Jesse Keith Butler,** and **Laura Vogt**.

Reptiles and birds take centre stage in 'Down Alligator Alley' by **Bridget Boland** and 'Aria of the Birds' by **EJ Nash**, while 'Take My Hand: Sleep With One Eye Open' by **Mel Anastasiou** and 'Footnotes to Wonders' by **Mark Budman** give us time-lost ghosts and fairytale character.

Meanwhile 'Fasteners', a graphic short by **Michaela Chan**, invites us to spread a towel out across the sand, open this issue to whatever page calls, and enjoy a great read.

FOREST OF SHADOWS

Matthew Hughes

Matthew Hughes writes fantasy, space opera, crime fiction, and historical novels. He has sold 24 novels to publishers large and small in the UK, US, and Canada, as well as 100 works of short fiction to professional markets. Matt has won the Arthur Ellis Award from the Crime Writers of Canada and has been shortlisted for the Aurora, Nebula, Philip K Dick, Endeavour (twice), AE van Vogt, and Derringer Awards. He was inducted into the Canadian Science Fiction and Fantasy Association's Hall of Fame. His magnum opus, What the Wind Brings, winner of the 2019 Endeavour Award, is available through pulpliterature. com. Pulp Literature also published his short stories 'The Devil You Don't' and 'Fishface and the Leg' in Issue 13 and 'The Bicolour Spiral' in Issue 26. Find out more about Matt on Wikipedia at Matt_Hughes_(writer).

Forest of Shadows

Valladio was a *fattoria* — an olive-growing farm — on a steep hillside, rows of olive trees climbing to a wire fence that separated the land from a mass of trees far beyond and above. Iron gates led to a dirt driveway winding up through the trees to end at a marble-paved courtyard ruled by two palm trees. The two-storey house stood brilliant white in the sunlight, with a separate smaller structure off to one side.

The bottom of the villa was a thirteenth-century farmhouse, and a second storey had been added in the 1920s. The palms were said to be a present from Mussolini, who used to come to shoot boar in the *Foresta Umbra*.

"*Foresta Umbra?*" Magda said.

Cecelia Chapman, the Englishwoman for whom Magda and Derek had come to housesit, gestured to the trees upslope. "The 'shadow forest'. A survival of the ancient forest of southern Europe, never clear-cut." She shivered a little.

She had them put their bags in the smaller building, once a mediaeval dovecote, now a tiny two-storey apartment. They would live there while the main house was rented out to tourists once the season began.

They came out to find Cecelia joined by a ruddy-faced fellow just entering middle age and a little boy of perhaps five.

"Gregory," the man said. "How'd you do?"

The boy was not introduced, nor did he appear to wish to be. Magda thought him odd: a triangular face, coppery curls, and pale, oddly shaped eyes. He regarded her with a detached air.

Downstairs, the villa had high ceilings and smallish rooms with tiled floors and a modern kitchen. Upstairs was a grand chamber leading to French windows and a balcony that overlooked the trees, adjoined by a lounge, master bedroom, and bathroom.

"Beautiful," Magda said, surveying the long dining table and the fine old cabinets with good china on the shelves.

"We've liked it," said Gregory.

Magda couldn't help asking, "Then why are you leaving?"

She saw something shift in Gregory's gaze, then he launched into an explanation: falling prices for olive oil, even the fine *Leccino* variety Valladio grew. Something to do with the creation of an 'olive oil lake' under the rules of Europe's single market and accompanying chicanery. Cheap Moroccan oil imported in bulk, bottled in Milan, and passed off as genuine Italian.

The Chapmans, Gregory said, had to go back to Britain and shore up their market. It meant abandoning, at least temporarily, their Italian *fattoria*.

"For which," he finished, "we undoubtedly paid too much."

They unpacked in the upstairs of the dovecote, accessed by a spiral staircase of black iron. A door led out to the slope, where stone terraces climbed upward, once apparently used for growing vegetables, long since gone wild.

As Magda turned to re-enter their bedroom, she noticed something carved into the marble lintel above the door. Old, she thought, and eroded by time.

She ran her hand over its smoothness. It appeared to be a man's head, wreathed in oak leaves, the features mostly worn away and hard to distinguish in full southern sunlight.

She took off her sunhat and held it to shade the carving, saw a broad brow, a pointed chin, a suggestion of a sensuous mouth, curls of hair, and deep-set, almond-shaped eyes.

Then she was called away. Derek had found a hammock shaded by the trees from which it was slung. "Dibs," he declared.

The Chapmans gave them lunch of Italian bread, olives, creamy *Perla Nera* cheese, bubbly water, and then an orientation: written instructions for handling the guests who would rent the main building, and instructions for compiling the welcome baskets. Plus the schedule for the man who brought the water tanker to refill the cistern, the Wi-Fi connection details, and the keys to the almost-antique white Fiat Panda they would be driving.

Their hosts would leave the next day.

Derek said, "It all sounds fine. The place is beautiful. I'm surprised you can tear yourself away."

No response. Gregory ducked his head and picked an olive from the bowl. Cecelia stared straight ahead. The boy ate methodically, his jaw muscles bunching as he chewed. Magda realized she hadn't heard him say a word.

She leaned toward him and said, "Looking forward to England?"

The child looked up at her sideways, still chewing. He said nothing.

"He's not a big talker," said his mother.

They slept in the upper room of the dovecote, the mattress soft, the single window open to let out some of the day's accumulated heat. Magda awoke to light flooding in from a moon as high and bright as a silver coin. She got up to lower the wooden shutters but stood for a while, leaning on the sill, letting the cool air flow past her.

She could smell rosemary growing among the olive trees, so foreign and yet somehow perfectly right for the place. As she reached to close the shutters she heard a faint sound, the high, sweet note of a flute, distant.

She listened, but the sound faded, as if the flautist was moving away or going behind a hill.

In the morning, after the English left, they drove into the little town, found the *bancomat,* and withdrew some Euros to make sure their Canadian debit card worked here. Then to the *supermercato* for pasta and panini, eggs and milk, coffee, and ricotta cheese. The store's owner spoke to them in German. Magda shook her head, tapped her chest, and said, "Canada."

"*Ah, Canadese!*" A big smile. "*Benvenuta.*" He plucked a package of pasta from a shelf and added it to their basket. "*Gratis.*"

"*Grazie,*" Magda said. She wanted to say 'kind', but could only remember her high school French. "*Gentil?*"

The merchant smiled and said, "*Gentile,*" with the Italian pronunciation sounding like 'jen-teel-eh'. Magda smiled and repeated it.

At the *macelleria,* another cheerful "*Willkommen*" from the butcher, and yet another expression of sheer delight when Magda said, "*Canadese.*"

Derek had consulted the Italian phrasebook they'd found in the dovecote. He knew he could point and say, *questo* or *quello*—this or that—and hold up the requisite number of fingers. So they got two chicken legs and four lamb chops, and then the butcher indicated some small, dark sausages.

"*Cinghiale*," he said. "*Molto bene.*"

They took four. Later, driving back to Valladio, Magda said, "What do you think 'ching-alley' means?"

"The book's in the back seat," Derek said. Magda eventually found the word. "Wild boar. I don't think we're in Kansas anymore, Toto."

Two weeks into the sit, the cistern-filling truck came. The man backed up close to the raised concrete platform with its steel trapdoor and unhooked the big hose. He began to fill, keeping an eye on the gauge that told him how much water was rushing into the underground tank.

When he was gone, Derek said, "Did you get a good look at him?"

Magda had. "Do you think?"

"That he might be the father of the Chapman boy? Peas in a pod, allowing for the difference in ages."

"My, my," said Magda.

Several more days, and she said, "Cistern guy's dad—or could be an uncle—was pumping the *benzeni* at the gas station."

"I saw," Derek said. "And, you know, I think I saw another one, an old man, sitting under the trees in the little park."

They had been there a month, had got to know their way around town, swum in a little cove, learned rudimentary Italian, and come to accept that everything stopped at one o'clock and didn't start again until five.

"We haven't been to see the shadowy forest," Magda said.

"It won't be much," Derek said, "not like Clayoquot Sound."

The funny thing about the Forest of Shadows, Magda's first thought was, *is that there are no shadows.*

The road wound up the steep slope, through land long-ago cleared for farming, then suddenly entered the forest—from bright sunlight to pervasive gloom in a hundred metres. No direct sunlight penetrated the overhead canopy, the diffuse, directionless illumination creating a perpetual twilight. The trees, mature beech and oak, stood widely spaced like silent witnesses, trending upward as far as Magda could see, gradually fading into the gloaming. No undergrowth, the forest floor uniformly carpeted in leaf mould, all muted greens and browns.

She slowed the car and rolled down the window, cool air flowing over her. After half a kilometre, the terrain levelled and the road widened. She pulled over, stopped, and turned off the engine. Now she could hear birds, a miscellany of calls, though she could see nothing in the overhead dimness.

She got out and stood, listening. Beyond the birds, there was nothing to hear: no wind through the canopy, creak of a branch, or hum of an insect's flight. She clapped her hands, heard no echo. Like an empty cathedral.

She left the car and walked among the trees, touched the smooth bark of a beech. Her footsteps made no sound, left no mark in the firmly packed detritus formed over millennia. She went from tree to tree, seeing sameness; looked up, saw stillness.

Men hunted aurochs here, their arrows tipped with stone.

She stopped, turned. Where was the car? She didn't think she had come far enough to lose sight of it. She felt a sudden disorientation.

Don't panic, she told herself automatically. Now came a spurious memory: the original meaning of the word was the terror that could strike wanderers in woods, an irrational fear generated by coming near to the old god, Pan, who ruled wildlands.

Magda had been in forests: British Columbia's second-growth woodlands and the giants of the coastal rainforest. She knew what to do. Descend, find a game trail, follow it. She descended a few steps, saw a glimpse of white. But more distant than she expected.

And then, from the corner of her eye, motion. She turned and saw something moving in the distance.

A memory. *Mussolini came here to shoot wild boar. Cinghiale* were dangerous, feared nothing, had tusks that could rip flesh.

She sped up her descent, aware that all the birdsong had ceased. The silent air that had been cool now felt chilly. The hairs on her arms stood erect. She kept her gaze fixed on the little car, sidestepping down until she was brought up sharp against its metal solidity.

She yanked open the door, threw herself in, slammed it shut, and frantically worked the handle to roll the window up. Only then did she turn to look, half expecting to see a slathering wild pig charging toward her.

Nothing. She rolled the window down an inch, listened. The birds were still mute and the silence was loud, weighted with a whine of noiseless energy.

And then a note, far off. The flute again. Thin and high-pitched, almost keening.

It stopped. Magda realized she had been holding her breath. She let it out, started the engine, manoeuvred the car to point downhill. When she shifted gears, her hand shook.

Summer brought phenomenal heat. Magda drove into town for groceries, but when she stepped out of the air-conditioned *supermercato*, the heat swallowed her like a biblical furnace. She put the bags in the back of the Panda — an oven on wheels — and realized she couldn't get in. So she rolled down the windows and looked around for shade.

The only relief was an awning over a bar across the street. She crossed and then peered through the glass door. It was dark inside. *Must be cooler*, she thought. She pulled open the door.

The awning kept out direct sunlight, and an oscillating fan set high on the wall moved the air around. She went to the bar, drawing curious looks from a couple of men drinking espresso. The owner, a plump, tall woman with glasses, came down the bar.

Per favore, Magda said. *Aqua frio*.

"You know, love," the woman said, reaching into a cooler and coming up with a bottle of San Pellegrino, "nobody around here says *per favore*. Dunno why. They just don't."

It took Magda a moment to recognize she was being addressed in English, and in an accent she was familiar with from two housesits abroad.

"Australian?" she said.

"Too right," said the woman, "if you don't mind the cliché." She was Sophia from Melbourne. A teacher and a child of Italian immigrants, she'd come to Italy on an exchange program. She'd met her husband, Benedetto, in Foggia, beyond the forest.

"We fell for each other, so when the exchange was over, I married him. We've got kids, we run this bar together, and he makes bonzer pastries."

Magda took a sip of the water. "My husband and I are house-sitting at an olive farm—"

"I know," said Sophia. "You're a subject of conversation. Old ones are all for you. Canadians liberated this place from the Germans. Younger ones don't care. But nobody is *against* you. That's important."

It hadn't occurred to Magda that anyone might oppose their presence. She finished the water. "I'd better get the groceries back before the butter melts to a puddle." She fished in her purse for coins.

Sophia waved a dismissive hand. "My shout. Come again, and try Benedetto's pastries."

Most evenings, a cool breeze flowed down from the forest. Magda and Derek took to sitting on a marble bench in the forecourt of the big house, talking about the day that had been and the ones to come. They drank the exceptional coffee that seemed to be fundamental to Italian existence and ate Benedetto's pastries.

"Do you hear that?" she said, one evening.

"Hear what?"

"Music." She canted her head from side to side. "Some kind of flute, but I can't tell where it's coming from."

Derek shook his head. "A radio?"

The melody swelled. It was almost familiar.

"You can't hear that?"

He shrugged. "We've got the six Norwegians arriving tomorrow. Did you put together a bigger basket than usual?"

Magda wanted to strain to hear the music, but practical matters intervened. "I got half a *Perla Nera*, bread, oil and vinegar, and some of those little almond cookies. Plus a bottle of *primitivo*."

"Six people, maybe two bottles."

"All right."

They fell silent, sipped their coffee. The music was gone. She felt oddly bereft.

Midsummer. They'd had French tourists and English. She'd enjoyed regular swims in a little cove, but now it was overrun by naked German tourists. Whenever she cleaned up after a party of guests left, she took to driving deep into the *Foresta Umbra*, each time going farther until she felt an impulse to stop, get out of the car, and experience the dim coolness of the place.

Sometimes, she stood silent among the trees. The third time it happened, she realized she was listening for the music. But it never came. For a brief moment, she felt resentment, as if she was being teased.

"Silly woman," she said to herself.

Derek had found a book in some collector's marketplace and had it sent through the post. It was an English translation of a slim volume written by a Frenchman in the 1950s and translated by a British university press. It was an accompaniment to a fairly successful novel — it had won the Goncourt Prize — set in a made-up coastal town that was obviously based on Porto Vecchio.

As a young man, the author had visited the area during Mussolini's reign. He'd been fascinated by the social milieu of a town isolated for centuries. Feudalism had survived: a trio of powerful families owned the best land for olive-growing and ruled unopposed, while their labourers and servants came from the nobodies who lived on the worthless sandy soil of the *luongomare*, the seashore.

Then EU money paid for seaside roads and resorts, putting the nobodies on top.

"For centuries," Derek said, "nothing changed. The villa we're looking after was owned by one of those big families. Apparently, they even practised *droit de seigneur* on the peasants' daughters. Then ... revolution."

"Weird place," Magda agreed.

Magda took up the little book when Derek had finished with it. She thumbed through the pages; the author had included hand-drawn sketches of sights he found interesting.

"Look at this!" she called to Derek.

He came to where she was sitting in the palms' shade, the book open on her lap. She held it up, spread-eagled. "Look."

He leaned down, peered. "Okay. So?"

"It's the face," she said, "above the door, with the leaves."

"So it is," he said, and his own face said, "And ...?"

"Look again. This one is not all weatherworn. You can see the features."

"So?"

"It's the water guy. And that old man downtown." Then it hit her. "And the Chapmans' kid."

There was no colour to the image. But probably the original sculpture wasn't white marble. The ancients used to paint statues with lifelike, sometimes garish, colours, but Magda's mind could add the brownish skin, the pale, slanted eyes, the wispy, tawny beard.

"It's old," she said. "The same face from hundreds — maybe

thousands — of years ago."

"An isolated place," Derek said. "Musta been a lot of in-breeding."

"Boy wasn't inbred, was he? Maybe that's why they wanted out. Lady English Iceberg must have melted somewhere around here. Embarrassing."

He laughed. "Maybe something in the water."

By mid-August, the heat lay upon the villa like a smothering blanket. The thermometer fixed to the wall of the dovecote rose above forty degrees, day after day.

The water in the cistern was getting low, and Magda was glad to see the tanker rumbling up from the gate. She went and found the Frenchman's book. When the hose was connected and the water flowing through the hatch, she brought the book to where the driver stood beside the tanker's control panel.

"*Guarda*," she said, holding the book open at the sketch of what she had begun to call the 'forest guy'.

The driver looked. His face took on an expression she couldn't define. He shrugged.

Her Italian was still rudimentary, but she had prepared. "*Dove posso trovare?*" Where can I find?

Now he gave her a sideways glance — a measuring look, she thought.

"*La Foresta*," he said, gesturing with a thumb over one shoulder. "*In alto*."

Alto meant high. "*Statua, scultura?*" Was there a statue, a carving?

He laughed and said nothing, though his face implied she had said something silly. The expression made his resemblance to the sketch even more striking.

She brought out another phrase she had learned: "*Voglio vedere*."

I want to see.

"*Vedere?*" said the water man and laughed again. He said something more, a rattle of words in the local dialect.

She signalled her incomprehension. That only made him laugh again. "*Vai a trovare,*" he said, then turned his attention to the flow meter that counted the litres going into the tank.

Go find out.

She climbed the marble steps that led to the terraces above the dovecote. Derek was lying in the hammock, inert. She told him what the water man had said. "I want to find it."

"Why?"

"Something to do. Are you just going to lie there?"

"Hot," he said. "Wait until evening."

Then it would be dark in the forest. "No. Come with me."

He closed his eyes. "Too hot."

She was prepared. She had bought a canteen and found a gnarled wooden staff in the dilapidated, roofless barn down by the gate. And she had bought a packet of Post-it notes — bright yellow — from the stationery store in town.

The forest stretched up and over a great massif that jutted out into the Adriatic like a tumour on the back of the leg that was the Italian peninsula. She had never driven all the way to the other side, where the woods ended in sheep pasture, flocks guarded by aggressive donkeys. Now she pushed the little Panda up steep slopes and navigated hairpin turns. She had the window open, hoping for cooling air, but it was almost as hot in the woods as at the villa, sun-heated air seeping down into the forest from the naked land above.

High up, she stopped, got out, slung the filled canteen by its shoulder strap, took up the staff, and began to climb through the widely spaced trees. When she had gone several paces, she looked back, saw the car clearly, and climbed a little farther. She reached into her pocket, took out the Post-it notes, pulled the top one free, and affixed it to a tree. The yellow paper seemed to glow in the half-light.

She moved on, angling up the slope, pausing to mark trees with brightness. The air was humid, a weight in her lungs. She stopped to rest, leaning her shoulders against an ancient oak, and became aware of a deep silence: *Birds too hot to chirp*, she thought. Then, as she was applying a note to the oak, she heard the flute again.

She stood, listening, turning her head to try to determine which direction the music was coming from.

Up, she told herself. She climbed some more, the ground steepening so she had to lean on the staff to propel herself higher. Sweat trickled down her back. She stopped, sat down, and drank from the canteen. The notes came again, a descending trill. *And not that far away.*

An image came into her mind: some rustic shepherd boy, sitting on a rock and playing to his animals, faithful dog at his feet.

She drank from her canteen again, but the water had gotten warm. The trees swam in her vision, and she wiped a sleeve across her eyes, felt the sting of salt.

It's okay as long as you're sweating, she knew. *It's when you stop sweating that you're in trouble.* She didn't know where she had picked up that piece of information about heatstroke, but it sounded right.

Need to rest and cool down. She looked up the slope. It seemed to level off a little to her right. She set the staff in the leaf mould, levered herself up, and went that way, taking it slow. She came to the level, and let out an "Oh!" of surprise and relief. It was a terrace built into the slope, surrounding a declivity filled with water.

Magda went to the pool's edge, knelt, dipped her cupped hands into it, and poured water on her head twice, then a third time. The liquid was cooler than the air. The effect was immediate. The muzziness that had been creeping up on her was pushed back.

I was pretty far gone.

The warm air wrapped itself around her again. *I need to cool myself properly.*

She rolled over, pulled off boots and socks, and put her feet into the water. *Nature's radiator,* she had read somewhere. Then she unbuttoned her shirt, unhooked her bra, and cast them aside. She pulled her feet out of the pool and slipped shorts and underwear off, then slid naked into the water.

It was not deep, nor cold enough to shock, but it raised goose bumps. She stretched and moved her arms to dissipate the warm layer her body heat built between her skin and the liquid.

Must be a spring feeding this, she thought. She felt around but could not find its source. *More seepage than flow.*

She positioned herself so that the back of her head was at the edge of the pool, barely submerged, and moved her arms again. She closed her eyes, let out a long breath, and relaxed.

She heard the music again. It sounded closer. *I really should get out and get dressed,* she thought, *before I give Shepherd Boy the surprise of his life.*

And then she thought, *What if it's not a boy, but a man, or even two of them, and a naked woman is an irresistible invitation?*

She raised her head and listened. The notes wavered. *Not too close*, she thought. *I'll stay in a few minutes, get properly cooled down.*

She lay back and closed her eyes, kept the water moving gently across her torso. The goose bumps had gone. She was feeling better.

A little time passed. She opened her eyes, found she was gazing up the slope that continued above the terrace and its pool. More trees, more leaf mould. But something else, several meters above, hard to bring into focus in the dimness. She sat up.

Well, I'll be, she thought. *There you are.*

It looked to be a pillar, with a head carved into its top—a particularly shaped head, the features all too familiar. *Found you.*

The music came again, still distant. She lay back, listening to it, enjoying a sense of triumph. A quest, hardship, discovery, and soon her return to declare her victory. A good day.

She slid into sleep.

She awoke from a dream that fell into tatters and fled as she tried to recapture it, leaving her with a half impression that it had been charged with erotic content. She sat up, sinking into the pool until her buttocks rested on the bottom and the water covered her breasts.

She had no idea how long she had slept, but her body was well cooled and the light seemed even dimmer than usual. She climbed out, used the edges of her hands to scrape the wetness from her, then got dressed. Downslope, she could just make out a yellow spot on a tree.

Better get going.

But she didn't. She refilled the canteen from the spring water then took up her staff, circled the pool, and climbed up to the pillar. Brighter light would have helped, but she was sure that here was the face from the Frenchman's sketch. The head stood on a square pillar. Halfway down, a stone phallus protruded, its upper surface smooth, as if generations of visitors had reached out and rubbed their palms across the protrusion.

Magda remembered that similarly adorned pillars were common at intersections in ancient cities, the Greeks and Romans touching them for luck as they passed by.

What the hell, she thought, and encircled the shaft with palm and fingers. The stone felt oddly warm, but she put that down to her hand having been chilled by her long session in the pool.

She turned and stepped carefully down the mould-covered slope toward the Post-it note, then searched in the gathering dusk for the next one. As the dark came down, she spotted the faithful Panda, pale as a ghost.

Mid-October. The heat had gone, and there had even been some rain. "I'm late," she told Derek.

He looked at his watch. "What for?"

Sophia had had three children in Porto Vecchio; she directed Magda to a local obstetrician. The doctor spoke a few words of English and Magda's Italian had improved, so between them they were able to establish that she was around nine weeks pregnant and everything appeared normal.

After five years of trying to have children, Magda and Derek had not even achieved a miscarriage. They had each been examined, and the medical conclusion was that they ought to be capable. Yet somehow they weren't. Or hadn't been.

"When would I be due?" Magda asked. She was thinking she would need to get back to BC to re-register for health care and have family and friends to help with all the ramifications of being a first-time parent.

The doctor produced a cardboard wheel, moved some circles around, and said, *"La metà di maggio."*

The middle of May. The sit would have wrapped up by then, but there would be a waiting period back in BC before she could be covered by the provincial health care system. She would have to go earlier and leave Derek to finish up.

She was mentally calculating dates when it struck her. Nine weeks pregnant by the chart was only seven weeks since conception. August. That was when the great heat was on, the top floor of the dovecote sweltering at night, even with the wall-mounted cooler running. At the end of each day, Derek and she had both been totally enervated, he even more than she.

They hadn't made love. Not once.

She wouldn't tell Derek about the dates, but she told Sophia.

"You'll just tell him it's premature," her friend said.

"But—"

A shake of the head. "You fell asleep in the forest, didn't you?"

When the infant was born, the nurse laid him naked and warm on Magda's chest while they were still cleaning her up. She looked down, saw the pointed chin, the wispy, coppery hair, the strange-shaped eyes regarding her with a calm and steady gaze.

Something in the water, she thought, then brought the little mouth to her nipple.

FEATURE INTERVIEW

Matthew Hughes

Pulp Literature: *We'd love to hear about the genesis of this story. I know you travel; were you in Italy when you began thinking about 'Forest of Shadows'?*

Matthew Hughes: Not while I was there, but it grew in the back of my mind. The actual location is Vallecoppa, an olive-growing fattoria on the edge of *La Foresta Umbra*. You can Google it. If you're really interested, you can book a stay. The forest is as I've described it. Quite unique.

PL: *Have myths always resonated with you?*

MH: Yes. In my teens, I was fascinated by Greek and Roman mythology. In my twenties, I dived into Joseph Campbell's Jung-influenced interpretations of worldwide mythology.

PL: *Your blog is great reading, and you're also a prolific writer of long and short fiction. How do you balance the two in your working days?*

MH: I've set my blog aside, after some kind of server update took it offline, but I post occasional biographical episodes on Medium.com. I've been concentrating more on self-publishing long-form fiction these days, aided by scores of Patreon patrons whose contributions help me to get by. I wrote 'Forest of Shadows' on an impulse.

PL: *If you could pick one place in the world to write this year, where would you go?*

MH: Ireland and Italy, alternating for the climates and seasons.

PL: *Thank you for taking the time to speak with us. What projects are you working on now?*

MH: I self-published a science-fantasy novel, *The One*, in May, and I'm writing a Dying Earth fantasy novel about a sorceress named Margolyam who was a well-liked supporting character in my short story series about Cascor, a kind of private eye in the far-future Old Earth, when science has dissolved and magic has come back. I should have the new book out in early July.

Select Bibliography

Matthew Hughes has published more than thirty novels. Here are the most recent.

The One, 2024
A God in Hiding, 2023
Cascor, 2023
Modie, 2023
The Ghost-Wrangler, 2023
Ghost Dreams, PS Publishing, UK, 2022
Passengers & Perils, 2022
Baldemar, 2022
The Emir's Falcon, Shadowpaw Press, 2022
Barbarians of the Beyond, Spatterlight Press, USA, 2021 (an authorized companion novel to Jack Vance's *The Demon Princes*)
What the Wind Brings, Pulp Literature Press, 2019

GRANDMA HAD GUNS

Finnian Burnett

Finnian Burnett's work explores the intersections of the human body, mental health, and gender identity. They are a recipient of the Canada Council for the Arts grant, a finalist for the 2023 CBC nonfiction prize, and a 2024 Pushcart nominee. Their stories 'Ethan's Pecs' and 'Nothing Left' appeared in Pulp Literature Issue 37, Winter 2023. And 'When Captain Picard Was My Dad' was our feature story for Issue 41, Winter 2024. When not writing or teaching, Finnian enjoys walking, Star Trek, and cat memes. Finn can be found at finnburnett.com.

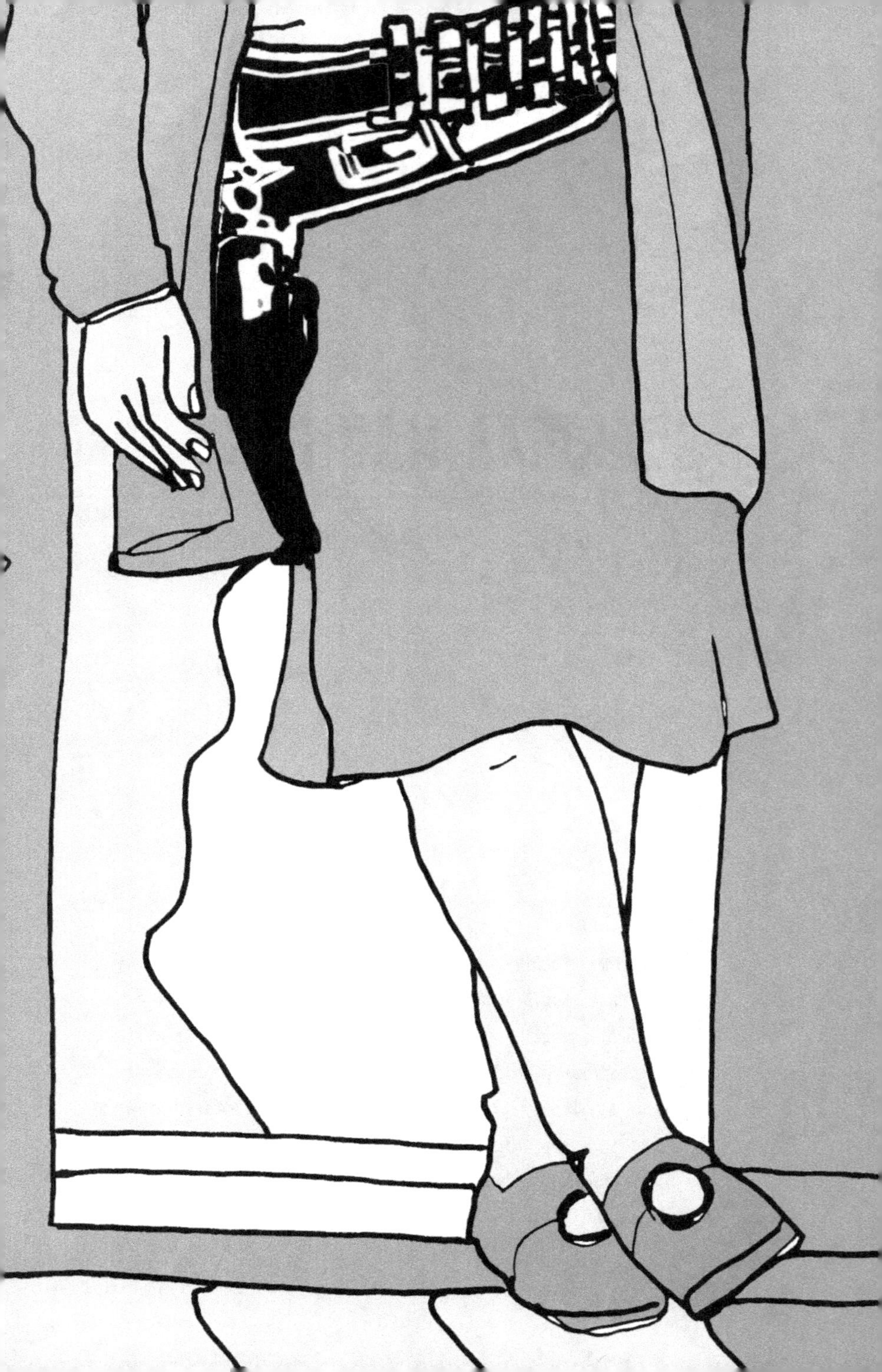

Grandma Had Guns

The monsters are here, my mom whispers in my ear, but they aren't monsters, nor gods either. *Just evil,* my grandmother said before they took her.

They're here to clean up the streets, my mom says loud enough for nosy neighbours to hear, though Grandma wasn't dirty. Grandma rushed the street one day, handguns drawn in each hand while the not-monsters were patrolling the streets. She charged right at the group of them while the rest of the townspeople cowered in their houses. Got one right in the eye, and wires sprang out from the empty socket, and the not-monsters laughed and pointed at the one with a gaping hole for an eye, laughed the whole time old one-eye was picking up Gran and throwing her into the back of their van.

No trial, no news, no chance to find out where she was taken or what happened to her, though my mom says Grandma should have known better than to shoot at them. They're tough on crime, Mom says.

Haven't been any rapes in town since they came—no murders, either. And the guy who used to flash us when we walked to school is gone, too. They cleaned up the streets, all right. Cleaned 'em right up.

The syndicate, people call them. *Tough on crime,* their leader said in speeches, and the town council voted to let them open shop in the abandoned purse factory on the outskirts of town on Bannerman Lane, where Tommy Darby and I used to ride our bikes and sometimes throw rocks through the windows.

The syndicate cleaned up the streets, my mom says, so loudly Mrs Plough looks at us. Mom is right. They've cleaned up the streets. They got rid of Allen McAllen, the guy who used to smuggle guns through town, up from sector eight. Allen used to be part of the local government, which is all the government we have left. Far as we know now, Allen McAllen is dead and so are the guys who used to work for him.

Mom pulls me inside. I lean against her comfortable bulk, and we peer out the window as the syndicate, or some of them, stride down the sidewalks. Their eyes track and scan. For a moment, one spies me through the glass. We stare at each other, and I wonder if this is the one Grandmother shot, though he has both eyes now, and if he wants revenge. My mother grabs my hand, gripping it so tight my fingertips turn white.

It's time, my mother says, more to herself than to me. And she pulls me into Grandma's bedroom. *Don't be stupid like Grandma,* she says, holding a finger to my lips to still my protests.

Grandma wasn't stupid; she was brave. Like the time Frank Curtis, the man who first brought in the not-monsters, knocked on our door while Grandma was cleaning the kitchen. She picked up the mop bucket and threw it in his face.

You want to clean up the streets? she'd yelled. *Use this.*

I'd laughed at Frank, covered with dirty water, but that night mom and Grandma got into a horrible fight and Mom threatened to kick Grandma out if she didn't stop putting the family at risk.

My mom touches my arm to get my attention. *They can be beaten,* she says. *Your grandma knew it, but she lost her mind, scared of what we have to do.*

She pulls the curtain over Grandma's window. She touches my cheek and when I look at her, she's crying. My stomach turns and I move to hold her, but she pushes me away.

Just look, she says. She touches a section of wall behind Grandma's bed, and it slides open. She pulls out a large suitcase, opening it on the bed. It's filled with guns: big ones, medium ones, and some so small I could probably pick them up in one hand.

It's time, Mom says again, and she hands me a gun, just a small one. It fits nicely in my hand, and I put my fingers on it safely, not touching the trigger as I heard Grandma say dozens of times. *Don't point your gun at anything you don't want a hole in,* Grandma used to tell me, back before the syndicate came, before Allen McAllen disappeared, before other people started disappearing and folks had to choose between telling on their neighbours or being taken themselves.

There's something else. She hands me a journal and I flip through it, running my fingers over my grandmother's handwriting.

I look at my mom. *Am I supposed to go save Grandma?*

She shakes her head sadly. *You have to do something else.*

I pocket the gun and rush off, my mother's words ringing in my ears. It was Grandma, not Allen McAllen, who ran the gun runners. My grandma and her mother before her. Now me.

My legs burn as I pedal for the factory, the tails of my father's old coat flapping out behind me. I screech onto Bannerman Road, my lungs heaving, Grandma's tiny gun heavy in my pocket. They started gun running from sector eight, not to arm criminals, as everyone says, but to protect women. In sector eight, women go to readjustment camps to rebuild society. Grandma and Allen were smuggling guns, yes, but more, they were smuggling women to safety.

As I approach the factory, my hands shake so hard my bike trembles under me. I pull around the far side of the building, where there aren't any windows, and dismount, burying my bike under brambles.

Under the windows at the back of the factory, I slide into a hole fifty feet away from the locked bay doors.

Just big enough for an underweight preteen girl, my mom said, and she was right, but it's so tight I have to hold my breath to get through.

On the other end, I bite my lip to keep from gasping.

Rows and rows of people, or whatever they are, hooked into alcoves, wires sticking from their heads. Some look completely human, others are missing arms, legs, or faces.

They know I'm here; I can feel it. Goosebumps crawl up my arms as I walk, then run, past the rows. The ones with eyes watch me but they can't move, that's what my mom said when she gave me Grandma's book, the one she'd been keeping about everything she and Allen McAllen discovered about the syndicate, the robots built by sector eight, the scouting team meant to wear us down before taking us over, and I'm panting as I run, crying, because I want to trust my mom and my grandma but I can feel the not-monsters, the robots, watching me.

I finally reach the main computer at the front of the building, a pulsating, living thing. I plunge my hands into the bulbous mass of wires and flesh, an oozing tower that parts before me and reveals a man.

He stares at me, dumbfounded. *You can't be here,* he tells me, and before I can respond, a metal hand grabs my wrist, shiny fingers wrap around me. The not-monster people start pulling from their alcoves. So much for Grandma's theory that once they were in a charge cycle, they couldn't move until it was complete. I reach around my body with my free hand and pull my grandmother's gun from my pocket.

Don't waste time shooting the syndicate, my mom had said, and I don't. I lift the gun and aim it at the man in the machine, and before I realize I've shot him, a pool of blood appears on his forehead and drips down his face. The robot arm falls from my wrist. The other not-monsters stop in their tracks.

Swallowing hard, I grab the dead man and pull him from the mass of wires and gelatinous muck. He comes away with a squicking sound that almost makes me puke. I toss him to the floor and lower myself into the seat he just occupied. Wires twist around my wrists and electrodes shoot into my forearms and my temples. The syndicate is in my head. They all turn to face me, and somehow, even the ones without faces look expectant, waiting for my orders.

I stare out at my new family, my not-monsters, the ones who will be hard on crime, hard on sector eight, the ones who really will clean up this town and every other town in this world. This time, I tell myself, as I stare down the long rows of minions, we'll do it right. This time, only the truly bad will be taken. *This time,* I repeat, and they all say it with me. *This time. This time.*

There's a new syndicate in town, I tell them, and they all move closer, seemingly eager to hear my orders. *And this time,* I say, *this time we're gonna do it right.*

THE GOLDEN MARE

JM Landels

JM Landels is the author of the bestselling Allaigna's Song trilogy as well as the spy novel The Shepherdess, currently serialized in even-numbered issues of this magazine. 'The Golden Calf' and 'The Golden Bull' in Pulp Literature Issues 39 and 41 were set in a different corner of Allaigna's world of the Ilmar. 'The Golden Mare' completes this short trilogy, and finds Saoira Little at a new turning point in her life. JM herself stays away from ruminants, but does keep a small herd of horses on which she teaches mounted combat at her school, Academie Cavallo, in Langley, BC. You can find @jmlandels on most social media platforms, or at jmlandels.stiffbunnies.com.

The Golden Mare

When the letter arrives, Saoira almost doesn't take the time to open it. Her saddlebags are already packed, and Mysa is hitched in the yard, tacked and waiting. The bulls-head necklet that Saoira never takes off told her yesterday evening that her son was sick or injured. She spent the night preparing, with only an hour or two for sleep.

She is so impatient to be gone that she needs to read the missive twice before the contents register. The meat of the letter is almost a relief: that Lennis broke his arm and a rib or two in a fall from his horse when hunting. He is not at death's door, and a broken limb will keep him from his duties while his head, which no doubt was rung in such a fall, has time to heal as well.

Reeth has been up most of the night too, and she puts a slice of fresh-baked bread and a cup of hot milk in front of Saoira. "Eat before you go, love. That's an order." She takes the letter out of Saoira's hand to read for herself. "It's not from the Duke." Allenis Andreg, Duke of Teillai, is Lennis's employer and, though he doesn't know it, his father. Reeth has never met Allenis, and Saoira herself has not seen him since before Lennis's birth. "Lauresa — isn't that his wife?"

"It is. Lennis is often posted with the Duchess's personal guard. But it's from Theiron, not Teillai."

"That explains why it got here so fast. Theiron's a day away, not three. But why's he there?"

Saoira chews a mouthful of bread, neither noticing the moist warmth nor tasting their best butter and Reeth's superior plum purée spread lovingly on top. She is too busy combing her memories for a clue. "Lauriana," she says at last. "Allenis's second daughter is married to the Duke of Theiron's son, I think. The Duchess Lauresa must be visiting her."

"Well, she writes that Theiron's best doctor is attending Lennis, who is resting comfortably," Reeth says. "Are you sure you won't take the coach and arrive dry and rested?"

Saoira dismissed that idea hours ago. "The coach takes the Næyvan road and won't arrive till late tonight. The south way is faster. And Mysa needs the exercise."

With a quick embrace and last-minute reminders that Reeth doesn't need—she's been helping Saoira run the dairy for more than two decades—Saoira sets off for Theiron in the driving rain.

Coming to riding late in life as she did, Saoira has a wariness that has never quite left her. That caution is amplified by the knowledge that Lennis's injuries were caused by a horse. With every lengthy stride her well-bred courser Mysa takes, Saoira imagines the mare slipping on the wet cobbles of town or the greasy mud of the south road to Theiron, which is little more than a cow track that skirts the Valnirata borders. There is peace now, thanks to Allenis's eldest daughter who sits the throne in Rheran on the other side of the vast Greatwood. Nonetheless, a lifetime of avoiding Ilvani territory is as ingrained as her caution in the saddle. These three worries—her son, the footing, and the territory—circle her so closely that she barely feels the rain that pelts her face and soaks through her waxed riding coat.

With her eyes on the treacherous ground below and the dark woods on either side, she fails to see the wagon blocking the narrow road until Mysa spooks at the mud-covered man crawling out from under the axle. The mare plants her feet, then jumps sideways, and Saoira tumbles from the saddle to the muddy ground. As she hits, the wet rein pulls from her wet glove, and Mysa spins and sprints back up the road towards home.

The mud-spattered man who'd scared Mysa is standing now, offering her a hand. "Are yeh all right, mistress?"

She doesn't reply, and doesn't take the hand, instead releasing a string of curses as she rolls to standing. She's furious at the man, at the horse, and at herself for choosing her green and flighty filly over her slow but steady old mare for the sake of speed. She forgets her worry about dark woods in neutral territory, and races back up to the bend in the road.

Saoira is just in time to see Mysa's retreating rump disappear around the next turn, flapping stirrups driving her onwards, her wet tail streaming behind. One tiny portion of Saoira's mind pauses to admire the speed of her young courser before the next waterfall of epithets emerges.

She feels a hand on her shoulder and spins around mid-curse.

"Will she stop soon, d'ye think, mistress?"

"That green idiot will gallop all the way back to Littlewater." It's already mid-morning. By the time Saoira walks back and retrieves her horse the day will be half gone, and her son will still be lying injured in Theiron. It's not just the rain that wets her face as she gazes at the faint bright spot behind the clouds marking the sun's progress.

"I'm so sorry, mistress," says the man, who, now that the rain has washed some of the mud from his face, is younger than he first seemed. Around Lennis's age, she thinks with a stab of pain in her heart that overwhelms the growing one in her hip.

"If ye can help me get my wheel back on, I'll see if I can turn this rig around and give you a ride back up. Perhaps she'll stop to graze before she gets to Rillonna."

Saoira looks at the wagon, its right wheel lying on the side of the track, and calculates whether the pair of draught horses will be able to negotiate that turn on the narrow tree-lined track with a seven-cubit wagon. They'd have to unhitch the horses and turn the wagon by hand.

She shakes her head. "Are you going to Theiron?"

"I am." He brightens, his wide smile a ray of light in the rain. "I'm meeting my lady-love there. It's been three moons since I saw her."

"I'll help you get your wheel back on, and you can give me a ride to Theiron." She doesn't pose it as a request.

"What about your horse?"

"She'll find her way home." Or she won't, Saoira thinks. She's not sure what's worse: someone claiming her beautiful young mare and the saddlebags full of healing herbs and ointments, or Reeth's panic when Mysa arrives home riderless.

Despite her light frame, Saoira is wiry-strong from years of wrestling calves, churning butter, and forking hay and dung. She's also repaired just about every bit of farm equipment she owns at some point or other in her life. So it's quick work to help the young man get the beautifully crafted wheel back on and replace the pin from the supply of parts kept in the wagon.

The wagon itself is a thing of beauty — its polished boards a variety of greens that match the surrounding forest, and its interior a marvel of ingenuity to create a comfortable home out of so tiny a space. She compares it to her holdings — the acres of land she owns and the grazing rights she leases, plus the original creamery, the dairy, and the new stone house she's had built — and she can't help but wonder if she and Reeth might not be happier with nothing but a wagon and a pair of horses to pull it. Without the work that comes with two hundred head of cattle, and the responsibility for a dozen staff to run the farm, the shop, and the house. And of course, without the wealth. But it's not gold that keeps her in business — it's care. She is proud of her herd and the excellent life she gives them, proud of the Littlewater cheese and butter that feed much of southern Aerach, and proud of the care she takes of the land that supports them all. The Littles have been dairy farmers for as long as Littlewater has been a dot on the map. Their fortunes have risen and fallen, but Saoira has brought the business to new heights with hard work, some luck, and the patronage of the Duke of Teillai. She cannot let all that go.

Glaignen is the young man's name, which rings a distant bell in her mind. He invites her to ride inside the wagon.

"Certainly not," she replies. "I'm covered in mud and dressed for the rain. The footboard will do for me."

When she introduces herself, he recognizes her name. "Ah, I knew ye must be one of us," he says. "Mother Irdaign speaks highly of you."

"The Lady Irdaign is your mother?" The woman who began tutoring her in Leisanmira magic eight years ago is a noblewoman, former Princess High of Brandishear, and grandmother of Lennis's legitimate half-siblings. But of course she is Leisanmira as well, like this young man.

"Not my mother, no," he laughs. "It's but a term of respect. But ye must know that—you're Leisanmira yourself, are you not?"

She shakes her head.

"I'm sorry—I didn't mean to insult you," he says. "I know not all Ilmari consider Leisanmira blood a boon."

"Oh. No, I'm not insulted. I'm not of your people, though." Though she doesn't know who her father is, and she's long suspected Leisanmira blood in her veins.

"Your hair, your eyes, and the fact Mother Irdaign says you're at least half makes you one of us. You're on the safe list, you know."

"Safe list?"

"The wind blows this way and that within the Ilmar. At present we're tolerated well—welcomed, even, in most places. But when the wind shifts, it is always good to know there are holdings that are friendly."

Friendly. She hadn't ever considered it. Of course she's friendly, she supposes. Irdaign made sure of that when she invited—or perhaps compelled—Saoira to learn magic. It is logical and natural she would be deemed 'safe', but she can't help but resent the assumption. Another responsibility.

He seems to sense her discomfort and changes the subject. "I apologize for our pace. You seemed to be in some hurry, and Bess and Butter are a good deal slower than your fine courser."

Butter. Saoira touches her hand to the necklet that rests under her shirt collar. It was made from her bull Buttercup's hide and enchanted with his blood and her own flesh. The thought makes the scar where her left breast once was ache with the memory of nursing Lennis. "My son," she says at last, "lies injured in Theiron. A hunting accident."

"My condolences, mistress." Glaignen places a comforting hand upon her muddy knee. "Might I surmise that if he's hunting at this time of year he would have access to the Duke of Theiron's physicians as well as his game rights?"

"That's a very polite way of inquiring whether he's a poacher. Yes, I believe he was carrying out his duties as a member of his garrison. I would hope the Duchess would extend him the courtesy of her doctors."

"Well, we'll try and make our best time for you, mistress." He gives the reins a slap, and Bess and Butter lumber into a slow trot, unconcerned by the rain or the mud.

The rain has stopped by the time they reach the lowlands around midday, and the high Una sun boils the water from the backs of the mares in great clouds of steam. Saoira sheds her wax coat and hangs it on one of the several hooks that adorn the front of the wagon. The seams have soaked through to her worsted shirt. The sun will have to dry that on her back, since her change of clothes, along with her medicines and her lunch, left with Mysa. Her stomach rumbles at the memory of the excellent cheese and loaf of Reeth's fresh bread. And then worry grips it again at the thought of Reeth greeted by the riderless Mysa. She must get a message to her.

Glaignen appears to have heard her stomach. "Take the reins, if you will, mistress. I'll get us some victuals from the wagon."

It's been a long while since she's driven her own wagon, which only ever has one beast pulling it. Still, she makes a competent enough show of dividing four reins between two hands and not interfering with the team of mares, whom she suspects would trundle steadily down the road with no guidance at all.

Glaignen emerges from the wagon with a wineskin and two small loaves. "When we find a commons, I'll let the girls stop to graze, and I'll heat up some soup, but this will keep us going in the meantime." He gives her a wink that makes her feel like a woman half her age.

The loaf is stuffed with lentils, spinach, salty cheese, and hot, unfamiliar spices that make her take more sips than she normally would of watered wine. But it fills her stomach, while the wine relaxes it, and she surrenders to the slow rhythm of the wagon.

The sun is hot by the time they stop in earnest to let the mares graze. Glaignen brings out a fire pot and heats a small cauldron of soup over it while he milks the mares. *Mares are such useful animals,* Saoira muses. *They can pull a wagon, carry you on their back, and still give milk, albeit less than a cow.* It seems foolish that most knights prefer stallions.

Glaignen is courteous to a fault as milker. Saoira would never dream of milking a cow while it grazed freely. But the mares are taller, and Glaignen doesn't need a stool. He simply follows the beast with a bowl in one hand, milking with the other. It strikes Saoira — who in this time could have filled a pail each from half a dozen cows, with twice as many tits per animal — as highly inefficient. But still, he spills not a drop, and returns with a full bowl of milk that he divides into two wooden cups.

He pulls out a second folding stool to place beside Saoira's and hands her one of the cups.

"You seem to be set up for company, with two of everything."

"My lady travels with me when her duties allow—which is not near often enough."

"You must be eager to see her," she offers.

"Indeed I am, but my haste has cost me. If I hadn't been pushing Butter and Bess through that rainstorm, I'd not have lost the wheel, and we'd both be in Theiron by now. But I would have lost the pleasure of your company." He brings his cup to hers.

"My own haste is my downfall—literally. If I'd chosen the steadier horse, or been travelling at a sensible pace for my skill, I'd not have been thrown. I'm grateful for the meal. And the ride." She takes a sip of milk and nearly spits it out. It doesn't taste bad—just unexpectedly sweet and thin.

"You don't like mare's milk?" Glaignen asks with a smile.

"I'm a cattlewoman, I'm afraid, all my life."

"Ah well, 'tis an acquired taste. Though better than goat or sheep, yes?"

"On that we agree." She brings her cup to his for another toast.

The second sip is not so bad, and she recalls tasting her own milk when Lennis was a babe. It's almost the same in colour, consistency, and sweetness. The reminder of Lennis makes her tear up.

"Don't feel you have to finish it." Glaignen hands her a bowl of soup. "It helps cut the heat of the spices, though."

"No. It's not that. It's my son—I can't help but worry." She brings a hand to her necklet, running a finger over the tooled indentations that trace a bull's head.

Glaignen looks at her curiously. "May I see your necklet?"

She starts to cover it with her collar—it's not something she shows to many people—but at last she remembers why his name is familiar. Glaignen was the name of the craftsman who made the necklet from the hide of her bull. She never met him, for her tree-priest dealt with finding and instructing a craftsman who could create the artefact in secret. But Irdaign had mentioned his name when she returned the necklet to Saoira and enlisted her as a student.

Saoira opens the collar of her shirt, and it feels like pulling apart her ribs and exposing her raw heart.

"Ah," he says.

"Do you remember making it?"

"I remember everything I make." His eyes drift down to her chest.

She's a small-chested woman, and she wears loose clothing. Few people seem to notice she has only one breast. His gaze seems to penetrate her worsted shirt and linen shift to the star-shaped scar beneath.

"Was it your son, the one who is injured, you had it made for?" Glaignen asks, his voice as gentle as the spring wind.

Bile rises in Saoira's throat, and she washes it down with too-spicy soup and too-sweet milk. If Lennis still wore the necklet, would he be lying injured in Theiron now?

She finds her voice again. "It was too powerful an amulet," she says. "Irdaign insisted it was dangerous for him to wear in the ducal household, where Mageguard might have noticed it. Irdaign promised that instead, she and her family would protect Lennis." It is unnerving, revealing these long-held secrets to a stranger, complicit though he was in the necklet's manufacture.

"But the Mageguard were expelled from Teillar half a decade ago. I should have given it back to him then."

Glaignen shakes his head. "It couldn't have stopped his horse from falling. But it told you he was injured before you received word, did it not?"

She nods.

"So there. It's working."

It doesn't seem worth arguing that the warning she received caused her a night's worry and put her on the road only a few hours earlier than the letter would have. Hours she has lost by falling off her horse. *Mysa.* Her mind flits back the mare. She feels sure she's home by now, and an idea strikes.

"Do you scry?" she asks. It's a bold question, and a word she'd never speak out loud in Littlewater. But they are alone here on the common, and if she can be considered 'safe', then she should be able to expect the same of him.

He nods. "Do you not?"

"I can look but not speak." Much like riding a horse, she learned magic far too late in life to be good at it. Weather sense, healing and mending, watching her herds — the skills useful to a dairywoman — those she can manage. "I need to get a message to my wife."

Reeth isn't exactly her wife, but 'business partner', 'staunchest friend', and 'invaluable helpmeet' all seem more cumbersome to say. Marriage is something the nobility use to secure inheritances and alliances. It's never been something Saoira has considered.

Glaignen rinses the milk bowl and fills it with water from the large cask strapped to the back porch. He sets the bowl down in the shade of the wagon and beckons Saoira to kneel beside him.

"Blow on the water," he instructs. "Hold your wife in your thoughts, and call her name." He places a hand on Saoira's shoulder, and it tingles with magic. "Now look for her in the water."

At first she sees only their shadowed heads haloed by blue sky in the settling ripples, but then a third form appears. She knows the back of Reeth's head like the back of her own hand. She stops herself from reaching out to touch the water.

"Reeth," she calls again.

Reeth pauses her hurried motion and cocks her head, then goes back to what she is doing. It seems she is currying a horse.

Saoira hears Glaignen's voice in her ear as if from far, far away. "Pull back a bit. You're too close."

She does, afraid that any movement will cause her to lose whatever tenuous thread connects them. She can see Reeth is grooming her fat buckskin cob, Cassie. Over Cassie's withers she can see Mysa, untacked, with a straw-stuffed blanket to dry her off as she stands eating from the manger. The rush of relief Saoira feels nearly does break the connection, but the swelling of love and gratitude for Reeth pulls her back. Saoira knows that if their positions were reversed, and Cassie had come home riderless, Saoira would likely have set out immediately on the spent horse in search of her partner. But Reeth, ever-sensible Reeth, has taken care of Mysa first, and is saddling her own much steadier mare.

"No ..." Saoira says. "Don't follow me."

Reeth pauses again, but then lifts the saddle onto Cassie's back.

"She can't hear me," Saoira murmurs to Glaignen, panic creeping into her voice.

"Try to relax," he says. "You feel what she feels, and she feels what you feel. You're magnifying each other's worry. Instead of telling her not to follow, give her a reason to stay.

"All is well," Saoira says to the water. "I'm safe. Stay home, look after the herd." She thinks, but doesn't say out loud, *I love you,* worrying that love might draw Reeth to her.

Reeth turns fully around as if searching for something. Saoira can see the red and puffy eyes that belie her dry face. Reeth seems to remember something and heads back to the house, leaving the horses tied at the manger. As the door to the house closes, the image slams to black.

Saoira sits back on her heels in frustration. "The wards," she says. "Irdaign helped set them around the house years ago. It seems they work." *Damn the woman,* she thinks unfairly. *Look where your help has got me.* "Thank you anyway," she says to Glaignen, unable to keep the note of despair out of her voice.

"You've given her pause," Glaignen says. "She may not know, but I believe she suspects that you're safe."

It is well past nightfall on this late spring day when the wagon rolls up to Theiron's gates. Glaignen gives his name, and the woman on watch bows and then calls for a sleepy-looking boy from within the gatehouse.

"Run to the castle. Tell them Prince Glaignen has arrived." She turns back to Glaignen and bows again. "I'll have the gate up for you in a trice, Your Highness, and I'll order up an escort."

"No escort, thanks," replies Glaignen with an easy smile. "I know the way."

The watch disappears into the gate tower, and the clank and rumble of chains starts up the process of swinging open the outer gates and lifting the portcullis.

"Prince?" Saoira looks at Glaignen.

Glaignen shrugs. "Not officially. It's a term Ilmari throw around, but I've never had a crown sat on my head."

"Just who is your wife?" Saoira demands, but her words are lost in the noise of the portcullis clunking into its upward rest. Glaignen slaps the reins on the rumps of Bess and Butter and hurries them through the outer and inner gates.

The wagon is about a third of the way up the high street towards the keep when they're met by another woman, this one out of breath from running hard. Her black hair is unbound, and she wears a long leather coat, unbuttoned, over an embroidered gown that has been tucked up through her waistband, revealing unlaced boots.

"You're late," the woman says.

Glaignen tosses the reins to Saoira and springs from the footboard. Saoira scrambles for the reins, drops one, and ends up pulling Butter's head into Bess's, setting off a mareish squabble as the horses come to a disorderly halt. Glaignen has locked the woman in an embrace, and he lifts her from the ground—no mean feat, since she's of a height with him.

"I'm sorry, love," he says at last, and then pauses for another kiss. "Wheel came off the wagon. But fortune delivered me help." He breaks from the embrace and sweeps his arm towards Saoira. "My love, this is Mistress Saoira Little. Saoira," he says, turning the woman towards Saoira, "my handfasted love, Allaigna of Brandishear."

Saoira's world tilts and spins, though less than it might have, for she felt a confluence of fates descending as they approached Theiron. So it is with relative equanimity that she stands, one foot on the tongue, the other on the spreader, and delivers a wobbly curtsy.

"Princess High," she says, her voice feeling cracked and old.

Glaignen's wife laughs. "Not here, not yet. My grandmother is Regent till I'm of age." Not yet twenty-five, with all the easy assurance of a woman twice her years.

"Your grandmother … the Lady Irdaign. We've met."

The princess cocks an eyebrow. "Is that so?" she says, but seems less surprised than she might.

"Are ye going to keep us chinwagging in the street, my love, or invite us into your sister's keep? These mares have been on the road all day." Glaignen leaps back to the footboard and holds his hand out for Allaigna.

"I'll ride the back porch," says Saoira, beginning to clamber down the off side.

"Nonsense," says Glaignen, and catches her by the wrist. "I've always room for a beautiful woman on each side of me."

Allaigna laughs and swings up, while Glaignen pulls Saoira back down beside him. There is indeed room enough for the three of them with Glaignen's arm around Allaigna. He starts the team forward, and the clatter of iron-shod wheels on cobbles drowns out all opportunity for talk. Which is just as well, for Saoira needs to sort her jumbled thoughts.

Allaigna, Princess High of Brandishear, is not just her mentor Irdaign's granddaughter. She is Lennis's half sister. For Lennis's father is the Duke of Teillai, and Allaigna is his eldest legitimate child. And here Saoira is, sharing a wagon seat with her. It is too dark to see Allaigna's features well, but she doesn't hear anything of Allenis in his daughter's voice, except for the slight Teillai accent. What she hears, as strong as the rush of the Littlewater in springtime, is the voice of Irdaign.

As they approach the castle gate, Glaignen asks, "Do you know where your son is being cared for?"

"The letter doesn't say. In the garrison, I suppose."

"Cared for?" asks Allaigna. "Is he ill?"

"He was injured in a hunt."

"Ohhh … Mother's pet guardsman. I'm sorry — I didn't mean that." She reaches across Glaignen and grasps Saoira's hand. "He's in the guest quarters," Allaigna continues. "It was an awful wreck. They had to put a bolt through the horse's head." That seems to upset Allaigna as much as anything. "But my sister's quite fond of the guard, and he's resting comfortably, I understand. I'll take you to him once we get the mares bedded."

It is somehow no surprise that this practical princess takes a hand in unhitching, rubbing down, and settling the mares in the stables. She even milks Bess while Glaignen does Butter. Saoira aches with impatience, but knows the importance of keeping a milked animal regular and comfortable. The bells chime midnight by the time the three of them leave the stables.

Allaigna directs Glaignen to her quarters and then leads Saoira towards the end of the second-floor gallery. She wishes Glaignen had come with them as a liaison between her and this high-born princess. She reminds herself of the days when she took the princess's father to bed and was utterly unabashed by his titles and his blue blood. She was younger, bolder, less wise then.

When they reach the door at the end of the gallery, the Princess of Brandishear turns to Saoira. "I think he's in this room, but I'm not sure. Let me check first." Allaigna knocks softly before opening the door a handspan, revealing light within. "Lauriana?" she says.

There is a movement — the sound of a chair scraping the floor — and a young woman, with a nose so like Lennis's it makes Saoira clap a hand to her mouth, sticks her head out the door. "Is Angeley here?" she asks.

Allaigna shakes her head. "You know it will be at least two days. Is that Mother's guard in there?"

Lauriana, Duchess-in-waiting of Theiron, steps into the gallery and closes the door behind her. She looks nothing like her pale-skinned, black-haired older sister. But Saoira wonders how anyone can see this young woman in the same room as Lennis and not know they are half siblings.

Lauriana hasn't yet noticed Saoira standing in the shadows of the gallery. "He's developed a fever. If Angeley's still two days away, we'll need to send for a tree-priest."

Saoira can wait no longer for polite introductions. "Your Grace," she says to Lauriana, "may I please see him?"

"Who are you?" Lauriana asks, noticing Saoira at last.

"His mother," Allaigna answers for her, reaching around her sister to open the door.

Saoira rushes into the room and freezes, struck by the tableau. At first she thinks it is Irdaign bending over the bed in which her son lies, applying wet cloths to his forehead and chest. But she knows it is Lauresa, wife to Allenis and mother to his legitimate children.

Saoira doesn't wait for permission. She rushes to her son's side and bends in a quick semblance of a curtsy before her knees fold completely and take her to the floor at Lennis's bedside.

She puts her right hand in his and places her left on his cheek. It is hot—so hot—and dry. "Lennis, I'm here, duckling."

His head makes a slight turn towards her hand, and he winces, pressing his hot cheek against her cold hand. Touching him at last, she wants to burst into tears with the relief, despite the horror of his right eye, swollen shut with a livid bruise.

"Mama," he says through clenched teeth. His neck spasms, tendons strung tight.

"Sh, son. Rest." She strokes his forehead, more worried now than she's been the whole long day. "Did he fall on his face, or was he struck by a hoof?" she asks the Duchess, who sits across the bed, wringing out cloths.

Lauresa looks at Saoira with clear, calm eyes and shakes her head. "Neither. He broke his fall with his arm, and his fall broke his arm." She indicates his left arm, which is splinted and wrapped at the wrist. "The bruise on his face was from before. He said he encountered someone in the tavern speaking ill of Lauriana."

A bar fight, defending the honour of his half sister. "Was he punch-drunk when he rode out with you?" She has reclaimed her old indifference to nobility, but she still tries not to make her words sound like an accusation.

Again, that calm shake of the head. "He claimed a stiff neck but no other ill effects. And would not be denied the pleasure of the hunt. He was quite lucid, and sound of judgement." The last is said with a note of severity—a faint hint that Saoira should not think of reproving her.

"I beg pardon, your Grace. I am Saoira Littlewater. Forgive the lack of manners from a worried mother."

Lauresa, mother of six, reaches across Lennis's body and places a hand on top of Saoira's and Lennis's where they lie clasped. "I gathered." She smiles. "I'm pleased to make your acquaintance, despite the circumstances. Lennis is a valued member of our household."

Household. Not garrison. It warms and relaxes Saoira by a degree, until she revisits the notion that Lauresa may be aware of who Lennis's father is.

"Where is the fever coming from? Is the wound infected?" Saoira bends over her son and touches the hand of the splinted wrist. Though the fingers are swollen, there don't appear to be any telltale red streaks heading north of the splint.

"The skin is unbroken," Lauresa says. "He had a mild fever even right after the fall. Which is odd —"

"— because he should have been in shock. Cold, not hot." She is beyond caring whether finishing a duchess's sentences is impolite. "Lennis." She shakes her son's shoulder. "Have you any other wounds? Older ones?"

He moves his head in a barely perceptible nod and says through slotted lips, "Foot." And then he emits a soul-shattering groan while his whole body arches in the bed, his chest reaching ceiling ward.

A voice cuts through Lennis's moan: high, ethereal, yet clear as morning bells. It is a lullaby. The Princess Allaigna is standing at the foot of the bed, her mouth open in song. Saoira feels the wash of magic flowing from Allaigna's open mouth and across Lennis's stiff form. The tension in his straining muscles and tendons eases, his back sinks down into the bed, and his eyes close. A hand on his chest assures Saoira that although his breathing has slowed, it is steady.

She leaves his side and moves to the foot of the bed to place a bold hand on Allaigna's shoulder. "Thank you, Your Highness. I had no idea you were a spellsinger." Her hand is gentle but determined, and Allaigna steps aside.

"I am, but I'm no healer. Has a tree-priest been sent for?" she asks her mother.

Lauresa's eyes are haggard as she begins reapplying cold cloths to Lennis's brow. "Yes, but Lauriana says she will arrive no sooner than morning. And Angeley is no closer."

Saoira only half listens to this exchange, for she has uncovered Lennis's feet and is searching them both. She finds what she has been dreading on the inside of his right heel, just at the margin of his sole. It is a small wound—no bigger than the head of a nail—but the flesh around it is hot and hard, and there are red streaks reaching up his calf.

"He can't wait till morning. The spasms will grow stronger. They could even snap his spine." She speaks with clinical calm that belies her bolting heart. "It is lockjaw. I think. I've seen cattle die from it." It is still hard for her to reveal her unsanctioned talent to these noblewomen. "And I've cured them."

Allaigna is looking at her with a raised eyebrow. "I did not know you were a tree-priest."

"I'm not. But I have learned some veterinary magic." *Thanks to your grandmother* is the part she keeps to herself. Trust only goes so far. "But I've only performed it on cattle. And when the wound is fresh. This is at least a quarter-moon old." Performing healing magic on an illness that has spread throughout the body could cost her own health. Or more.

"I'll need a bowl and a clean knife," she says. "And a promise. If I lose consciousness, you must intervene. Break the connection between my son and me so the healing doesn't flow back into me. Have I your word?"

She looks from mother to daughter. The former nods, and the other replies. "I can do one better. I can bolster your magic with my own."

Allaigna keeps Lennis resting in slumber with her lullaby, while Lauresa helps Saoira lay down towels, clean her knife, and position Lennis so his feet hang over the edge of the bed, with a bowl on the floor beneath them. Allaigna's lullaby is directed at Lennis, and she is a skilled enough spellsinger that there is very little drift. The magic pours straight from her mouth to his body, not just his ears. But Saoira can still hear the beautiful melody and needs to resist its invitation to sleep.

Lauresa smiles at her. "Hum a counterpoint." She demonstrates with a short arpeggio from 'Mistress Tomnelly', a bawdy drinking song. Saoira's no musician, but everyone in Aerach knows the tune well. It fits perfectly between the long clear notes of Allaigna's song, and its jaunty rhythm sharpens Saoira's mind.

"Are you a spellsinger too, your Grace?"

"No." Lauresa laughs. "But I've lived my life surrounded by them, and I have my defences." She gives a conspiratorial wink. "Are you ready?"

"Almost." Saoira unties her necklet and fastens it around her son's throat. She feels bare and vulnerable without it, but comforted as its magic settles into Lennis's stiff muscles.

She pulls a stool to the foot of the bed, puts one hand on Lennis's foot, and picks up her knife. Her mind is sharp with 'Mistress Tomnelly' looping in her head, but when she brings the tip of the knife to Lennis's heel, her hand starts to tremble.

"Would you like me to make the cut?" Lauresa asks.

Saoira looks into the calm eyes of the woman who should be her rival — whose own children should be threatened by Lennis's mere existence — and hands her the knife. "Three cuts, in the shape of a star. A finger width each," she says.

Lauresa nods, takes the knife, and with the assurance of a surgeon makes three perfect cuts. Lennis is so deeply asleep he doesn't flinch, which both comforts and worries Saoira. She takes back the knife, still red with his infected blood, and pricks her own finger with it. It is perilous to introduce the infection to her own bloodstream, but it is the fastest way to school her body on how to shape the healing.

Saoira closes her eyes and focuses on the throb of the knife prick, sending her thoughts rushing through her own arteries, exciting the healing elements within her blood. She places one hand on Lennis's wound and the other on his uninjured foot, creating a loop of healing magic that flows out her right hand into his foot. She visualizes it coursing through his body, chasing the infection, cleansing it from his muscles, nerves, and tendons, and drawing it out through her left hand like a poultice.

It is exhilarating, as always, this first rush of healing magic. It seems as if she is drawing energy from the air itself, like a lightning rod feeds the ground in a storm. And with the storm comes rain, the sound of Lennis's blood dripping into the bowl. The loop is running, but of course it is not closed. She feeds Lennis's body with her vitality, and draws the toxins out through the wound in his foot. She hardly feels Allaigna's hands settle on her shoulder, but she feels the other woman's song — changed now — resonate through her flesh, amplifying the arcana that runs through her blood.

But there is so much poison. The infection is everywhere. It will take all of her slight body to heal his. Her breasts ache — both the right and the phantom left one — with the memory of nursing him. Her womb, still these last years, seizes and cramps with the echo of labour.

Lennis's body spasms as she holds him by the ankles, and blood spatters in the bowl beneath his foot. She feels the pull of anima singing through her veins like lightning arcing off the wet rocks of the Giant's Head in midsummer, with a smell that fills and cleaves the air. And then it drains and flickers, leaving her body as her vision dims and blurs.

Saoira awakens to a voice she knows but can't place, singing. The air is warm and scented with herbs both familiar and strange. The bed is soft and smells of her son.

Lennis. Fear wells up as her last memories float back. Did she fail, and leave her son to an agonizing death? She moans.

The voice stops, and a cool hand touches her brow. "Saoira?"

She recognizes the voice. "Irdaign." Her mentor, and the matriarch of this family she has inserted herself into. She reaches up and clasps the hand pulling away the scent-laden cloth that was covering her eyes. Irdaign's face swims into focus. Saoira should thank her, for she knows with certainty this woman has saved her life. But that is immaterial compared with her concern. "Lennis?"

"Shh," Irdaign says. "Rest." When Saoira struggles to sit, Irdaign's firm hand keeps her in bed. "Lennis will be fine," she adds with stern emphasis. "You, on the other hand, need to rest." And with that, Irdaign begins to sing again, this time a lullaby much like the one her granddaughter Allaigna sang, and Saoira finds herself unable to defy sleep.

She slept for three days, on and off, she later learns. If Irdaign—Angeley, as her grandchildren call her—had not arrived partway through the second day, Saoira is not sure she would have awoken at all.

"You gave too much of yourself," Irdaign explains as she and Saoira sit on a sunny balcony off the sick room. "It's an easy thing to do when you love your patient. It's why we shouldn't treat our own."

"Lennis has barely been to see me," Saoira notes between sips of her tea.

"Ah, the ungrateful bairn." Irdaign shakes her head. "A grown man would feel embarrassed nursing at his mam's pap, would he not?"

Saoira opens her mouth to argue that it's hardly the same, but she allows that the magic felt much the same. Her phantom breast twinges, and she gives a sorry laugh. "I'll gladly stick to tending cattle, given the choice."

Irdaign changes the subject. "I sent a letter to Reeth. She's hired an extra hand to help with the herd. She'll be coming tomorrow to bring you home."

She's not a seer like Irdaign, but the older woman's words trigger a vision in her mind's eye. Reeth, lovely Reeth, riding the road to Theiron, the evening sun turning her dun mare to gold. Relief fills Saoira. She breathes in the steam from her cup, and lets the warm sun melt her.

Later that day, Saoira receives an invitation to dine with Lauresa. She should not feel as frightened as she does. The woman has shown nothing but hospitality and kindness. And yet the unspoken knowledge that Saoira birthed the Duke's son before his marriage to Lauresa was a month old sits like a stone ready to break off a precipice and tumble down, wreaking havoc on the lives below. Saoira holds the glowing image of Reeth, riding to her rescue on her golden mare, as a talisman in her heart.

The page who lets Saoira into the solar leaves, closing the door behind her. The Duchess Lauresa is seated at a small table already laden with food and a pitcher of cider. It appears there will be no servants here.

"Thank you," Saoira says to Lauresa, before it crosses her mind that she should wait for the Duchess to speak first, "for your care of my son." She attempts a curtsy, which is hard to make graceful when one is wearing trousers.

Lauresa smiles and gestures for Saoira to sit. "Cider?" she asks, pouring from the pitcher. When Saoira has perched herself on the edge of the chair, Lauresa continues. "Lennis has always been a favourite in our household. But I would do no less for any of my retinue. Did you know," she says in a conspiratorial whisper, "that Lauriana had quite the crush on him as a girl?"

Saoira gives a nervous smile. "He wrote that in his letters. He did nothing to encourage her, he assures me." She takes a sip of cider, and hopes the shaking in her hand does not show.

"Of course not. But she was always wilful with her puppy loves. I'm afraid I told her a lie or two about him having other attachments. I couldn't, after all"—she puts down her cup and gives Saoira a level gaze—"tell her he's her half brother."

Saoira swallows too quickly and the cider fizzes up her nose. When she has recovered her voice she asks, "Did he tell you that?"

"No," Lauresa's voice slows. "But if you think I wouldn't recognize my children's sibling—"

"Of course," Saoira replies too quickly, heaping the impoliteness of an interruption on top of all the others. "He looks very much like …"

"His father?" Lauresa finishes for her. She laughs. "I'm sorry, Mistress Little. I don't mean to make you feel uncomfortable. I found your letters to Allenis a long time ago. He keeps them under a floorboard in his chamber."

All the worry, all the sacrifices she made to keep Lennis's identity secret, were for nothing, then. She'd laugh if it weren't so tragic.

"I was angry at first," Lauresa admits. "I was carrying my older son at the time, and our marriage was at the warmest point it ever had been." She takes a sip of cider. "I don't think it's been warmer since." She shakes her head like a horse troubled by a fly. "But how could I be angry about a son conceived before we ever met?"

There is a weight underneath Lauresa's light tone, and Saoira recalls that Allaigna, the eldest child looks nothing like Allenis. She doesn't dare ask about that.

"Does the Duke" — she can't refer to him by name to his wife — "know Lennis is his son?" Saoira's heart is breaking all over again. She desperately wants Allenis to know his son, to love and admire the man he's grown into. And yet she can't let go of the fear she's held all the years Lennis has been in the Duke's service. That fear is not of the Duke, but of the woman seated before her.

Lauresa shakes her head slowly. "Allenis and I spend a limited amount of time together. And I have kept Lennis from attending me in those periods."

So his heritage *has* hindered Lennis's opportunities for advancement. The secrecy she forced him to swear to over the years, and the magic and flesh she has spent to enforce it, have done no good at all.

"Do you ..." Saoira forces the words past the burning lump in her throat. "Do you think he would dismiss Lennis if he knew?"

Lauresa laughs. "He'd have a hard time dismissing my personal guard without my permission. But he would be torn. He would want to acknowledge him. And that ... could be problematic."

For your own children, Saoira thinks, *who are all younger than Lennis.* She recalls the day Allenis proposed marriage and she declined.

She had no wish to become a duchess, to give up her cattle and her growing dairy business. But would it have been kinder to Lennis?

"All Lennis wants," she says, "is to see a light in his father's eye."

Lauresa nods, head bowed in sympathy. Or is it shame?

"For myself," Saoira says, "I want nothing but to see him safe." She doesn't need to add that safest would be retired from the guard and home with their herds in Littlewater.

"I haven't the power to grant him recognition or titles," Lauresa says, "but I can ensure he retains his position."

"Could you …" Saoira hesitates, wondering that she can ask so much of a duchess. "Could you ask Allenis"—the name burns on her tongue, but she uses it deliberately—"to acknowledge him privately, but not officially?"

Lauresa looks pensive. She is no doubt weighing the risk to her own children's positions if another son were to come to light. "I could. Yes. If it means that much to you that he knows."

"It means that much to Lennis." Saoira feels the tingle of cider and the warm spring evening fill her. "Thank you, your Grace. I owe you more than I can repay."

"You raised a fine young man who is a credit to our household. Thanks goes the other way." She laughs. "If my own son had been raised as a cowhand instead of a ducal heir, it would probably have done him good. And besides," she says, serious once more, "my husband deserves to know his son." Lauresa eyes Saoira up and down. "What about you? I have two lives, with a lover in Brandishear and a husband in Aerach. I would not mind if Allenis had a mistress."

Saoira's heart creaks and contracts in her ribs, recalling the deep friendship she once shared with him. She takes her time replying. "It was a chance encounter, when we met. His horse threw him and scattered my herd. By way of apology, he gifted me a bull calf of exceptional bloodlines."

"Generous," Lauresa murmurs.

"To a fault," agrees Saoira. "It was too large a gift where none was needed, and a heifer would have been less trouble for me."

"And so you were indebted." Lauresa frowns. "Did he use that leverage to coerce you?"

"No! Never that. It was many years of a growing friendship — letters, and thrice-yearly visits — before he stopped staying at the Duchess of Rillonna's palace and spent his nights at my dairy." She is hesitant to say the next part out loud but feels Lauresa has a right to know. "He asked me to marry him, and I said no."

Lauresa raises her eyebrows. "You would have been Duchess."

Saoira shakes her head. "You can dress a dairywoman as a duchess, but it won't change what she is. I was content with my life."

Lauresa is resting her chin on her fist. At last she looks up. "Would you take him back to your heart if he came to visit you? We have our heirs. I wouldn't begrudge him his first love …"

Saoira interrupts her once more, this time with a smile. "I would welcome your husband at my table to talk about our son or anything else he wishes. But …" She pauses, realizing for the first time in her life it is true, "I have a wife now, and she's riding here to bring me home."

§

For more high fantasy, family drama, and political intrigue set in the lands of the Ilmar, check out the spellbinding Allaigna's Song trilogy from JM Landels at Pulp Literature Press, pulpliterature.com/allaignas-song/

WATER IS NOT WHAT YOU THINK IT IS

Casey Killingsworth

Casey Killingsworth *has been published in numerous journals including* The American Journal of Poetry, Better Than Starbucks, The Moth, *and* 3rd Wednesday. *His latest book is* A nest blew down *(Kelsay Books, 2 0 2 1), and a new collection,* Freak Show *(Fernwood Press), is due out in 2 0 2 4.*

Water is not what you think it is

Water is not what you think it is

Who knows what the rule is for finding
a pile of bones in the middle of the forest
but I'm guessing it has to do with a pause,
you know, meditating about all the breathing
that goes on in the world, and then it stops.

I saw some bones once and remembered
some prayer about death and I tried
to run through it in my mind but
of course I forgot most of the words.

I'm trying to hang on, that's the part
I remember, but I'm going to fail
because that's why there are so many
bones in the middle of the forest.
We all fail. Amen.

FOOTNOTES TO WONDERS

Mark Budman

Mark is a refugee from Moldova who learned English as an adult. His work has appeared in publications such as Catapult and The Mississippi Review. In 2008 Counterpoint Press published his novel My Life at First Try. One anthology he co-edited, Short, Vigorous Roots, was the 2022 Foreword Indies winner. Kirkus Reviews awarded his latest short story collection a starred review and named it one of the best books of 2023. This story previously appeared on juked.com in January 2020.

Footnotes to Wonders

I. Humpty Dumpty in the Afterlife

After Humpty Dumpty[1] took a great fall and arrived at his next destination, the Devil[2] glued him together again, encrusted him with diamonds like a Fabergé egg,[3] inserted a straw in his shell, and glued him to his fireplace mantle. Now, Humpty Dumpty has to watch waterboarding[4] and other enhanced interrogation techniques of all the king's horses and all the king's men during the day. In the evening, the Devil slurps him out, all 78 raw calories of him, through a straw. In the morning, Humpty

---

[1] 'Humpty Dumpty' is 'Shaltai Boltai' in Russian. It means 'though we lost the Cold War, we can beat you in chess and hack into your records'.

[2] The Devil (from the Greek διάβολος, or diábolos slanderer or accuser) is commonly accused of forcing folks to do something not nice. Buy *The Devil Made Me Do It* on Amazon. Free shipping on qualified orders.

[3] In some languages, 'eggs' stand for the testicles, as in 'they kicked him right in his Fabergés'.

[4] Waterboarding is legal in Hell, but the Supreme Court of Hell hearing is upcoming in 3018.

Dumpty is full of high-quality protein, vitamins, and minerals again. The Devil calls him 'my little Sisyphus', though Humpty Dumpty stayed away from boulders from the day he was laid.

Humpty Dumpty[5] wishes he would fall one more time and break into a billion pieces, impossible to fix, but the glue is devilishly strong and the floor is covered by a thick Persian rug. So he is stuck. That is until he learns how to turn bad and cause the Devil a bellyache[6] no doctor can fix. Maybe then, the Devil will stay away from all high-cholesterol products.

Humpty is full of resolve. He's married[7] to the idea of revenge. He'll never chicken out. Neither in the afterlife nor beyond.

---

[5] Hard-boiled eggs is probably the easiest dish to make, not counting cereal and milk or a baloney sandwich. It's the food of choice for busy professionals in the next world.

[6] According to the US Food and Drug Administration (FDA), approximately 142,000 illnesses are caused every year by consuming eggs contaminated with Salmonella. How to wash eggs is a controversial subject for most ghost foodies and undead food inspectors.

[7] Marriage is a union of souls that takes advantage of female ovulation.

II. Healthcare, Exposed

About fifty miles up and west from Humpty Dumpty's current domicile, the Invisible Man married a Highly Visible Woman, and they had two kids: a girl and a boy. The girl took chiefly after her father. Few people have ever noticed her, except when she helped someone and they could see the result. And, oh, yes, when she turned the right way, and when the sunlight fell on her just so, they could see the faint outlines of her bleeding heart.

The boy took mostly after his mother. He was everywhere at once, the man of the hour, very handsome, a gifted orator,[1] a great cook, especially of devilled eggs, but no one could see his heart, even on ultrasound.

Their doctors[2] were puzzled, but the insurance didn't pay them to do something about it because they couldn't find the appropriate code.

One of the doctors, a board-certified cardiologist,[3] dug a hole in the ground and whispered this secret into it, but he was fined $50,000 for violating HIPAA[4] rules.

The boy posted "healthcare sucks" on Twitter and received 25,600 likes and one death threat.

---

[1] Someone who gets a lot of 'likes' on social media.

[2] A person who asks you a lot of questions for money and prestige. Alternatively, in Christianity: an eminent theologian declared a sound expounder of doctrine by the Roman Catholic Church — called also a doctor of the church.

[3] A person who wears a *Cardio is Hardio* sweatshirt at home.

[4] The forms you need to sign before posting your diagnosis on social media.

III. On Spider Mating

Not on this planet, but on the planet Hieronymus Bosch in the vicinity of the star Betelgeuse, 642.5 light years[1] from a board-certified cardiologist who has violated HIPAA rules, the Spider Man married Wonder[2] Woman. He wanted kids, but she was convinced that as part of its life cycle, the spider mother dies after she lays her eggs. Or, if she survives somehow, the kids commit matriphagy, or mother-eating.

"Imagine: a thousand babies eating me at once," she said mournfully one day, while they watched the sunset from a sheer cliff. "Do you want that?"

He turned his six devilishly bright eyes to her. "You'll be fine."

"It would take more than that to convince me."

Fortunately, healthcare[3] was free in that country, and the doctors were determined and pervasive, so they convinced her that she would be fine. And she was.

Her pregnancy lasted only a few days, she had only two wonderful, healthy babies, she didn't die, and they didn't eat her. But the Spider Man shrivelled and died a week after sex.[4] Happens to many man-spiders.

She placed his cremated remains on the mantel. The babies wove a nice sticky web around it, and whatever flies were caught they released into the wild on humanitarian grounds.

---

[1] The years of higher than normal sunshine. Alternatively, the years of easy living.

[2] From the Old English *wundor* (portent, horror; monster.), i.e., political opponents, creeping things, rotten eggs.

[3] Something that sucks on Earth but works wonders on Hieronymus Bosch.

[4] A strictly procreative activity in some circles and fun in other places.

ARIA OF THE BIRDS

EJ Nash

EJ Nash is an Ottawa-based writer. Her work has been published by The Globe and Mail, Nature, Woman's World, and CBC. This story earned an honourable mention in the 2022 Hummingbird Flash Fiction contest. When she's not watching the birds out the window, EJ can be found on X @Nash_EJ or at ejnashwrites.com.

$\mathcal{A}$ria of the Birds

The day that our dog Mark ran away from home was also the day I discovered why the blackbirds sang. For a mutt from the pound, Mark was an integral part of the family. When I listed my siblings, I named all three: Anna, Jason, and Mark. Only the first two were human.

That was the summer that melted the soles on our sneakers, the summer when the air slipped down our throats to choke us as we slept. Anna and I wanted to play a joke on Dad by trying to fry an egg on the hood of his car—and it worked. Lunch was eggs and bacon à la Ford. I picked out the little bits of grit that ended up in the yolk.

It was no surprise that Mark wanted to leave. We had no air conditioning, so our afternoons were spent haunting the mall and the arcade. When we came home, Mark would greet us lazily, a paw flicking with effort. And then came the day when he wasn't there at all.

The search party was organized. Mom and Anna combed the nearby forest; Dad and Jason went to the Humane Society to see if someone had brought in a dog with a scar over his left ear. I stayed at home in case he loped back.

The house was a mausoleum without anyone else. I imagined mould creeping up the siding, dust settling on furniture. I was ten years old and had never been left alone before. I wanted to scream, just to hear how loud I could be. As the middle child, I'd never had space for myself. Anna, the athlete. Jason, the scholar. And me — the girl left at home.

I took Mark's dog treats from the cupboard and used them as chalk on the driveway, hoping he could smell his way home. I envisioned an elaborate message: *Come home, Mark, we miss you.* But the biscuit only left a translucent, waxy residue on the driveway. I sat on the curb and wondered what to do next.

I imagined striking out on my own and finding Mark quivering on the tracks behind the warehouse on Elmvale. A train would blast towards my beloved friend, its brakes squealing uselessly — but I would whisk him away in time! There would be a ticker-tape parade. An award in my honour. Speeches, perhaps a medal or two.

The moment was so vivid that it took me a moment to notice the blackbird that had flown down to investigate the message on the driveway.

"Hello," I said. The bird cocked his head and hopped backwards.

I stood up. "I didn't mean to scare you."

The bird flew onto the road. He looked handsome, like a man wearing a dark suit. I blinked, and the bird opened his beak.

His voice! The first note melted the driveway into a glittering opera theatre. The man stood in the centre of a gilded stage, held his hands behind his back, and unleashed an aria that trilled in the air around me.

I was in the audience, enraptured. My dress was made of silk and honey; I ran my fingers across gold threads as I listened to the song that filled the concert hall. That soprano cry caressed my back and grew into wings. The song continued. I became the bird and burst through the vaulted ceiling into the streets of my own neighbourhood. Mark was behind the grocery store, happily snacking on spilled salmon. I waved my wing as I passed him.

My scream of joy became the most beautiful melody I'd ever heard. The world was a blur of colour and motion; an artist had streaked neon dyes across my vision. But the colours were musical notes — I could hear the shriek of vermillion, the laughter of lavender. The rainbow hues tasted like sugar.

I passed my school, downtown, even the border. I saw Hudson Bay and the St. Lawrence and the Labrador Sea. The chords were an updraft for my wings, carrying me farther. The old sailors were wrong; the North Star wasn't a celestial body. It was this harmony, this choir of colour and sound.

I was the singer, I was the song, and I heard my own voice: *I will be found.*

Diving into the Atlantic, I let myself drown. I would be the message in the bottle. The future girl who walked along the beach would find my story. She would clutch the song to her chest as she ran along the coast, the sand digging under her toenails. A reminder.

She would come later. For now, the notes sank into my bones as the undertow carried me to the shores of my house.

And when my feathers turned to flesh, when the ocean turned to salt and then asphalt, I knew that Mark had heard the blackbird too.

MIDLIFE KATABASIS

Jesse Keith Butler

Jesse Keith Butler *is an Ottawa-based poet who recently won third place in the Kierkegaard Poetry Competition. You can find his poems in a variety of journals, including Arc, Blue Unicorn, THINK, and flo. His first book,* The Living Law *(Darkly Bright Press, 2 0 2 4) is available wherever books are sold. Find him at jessekeithbutler.ca.*

Midlife Katabasis

In my fortieth year   When I'd mortgaged too much
In the crestfallen arc   Of a middling life
At the midpoint I turned   And walked to the water
I left the porch light   To spill onto the street
I'm not even sure   That I bolted the door
Past the mist of the lawn   Past the white webs of trees
There waited the river   In billowing night
I went to it wanting   I went to it ready
To follow it all the way down

The banks of the river   Were blanked out in darkness
As ground rose around me   The stars fell like cinders
My nostrils felt singed   With the smell of decay
And the water wound down   Past the roots of the buildings
A silhouette city   Leaned over the sky
And the water wound down   All its misshapen creatures
Awaited the deluge   To wipe us away
And the water wound down   And it gathered me with it
To flow with it up through the flood

The hulls of the yacht club   All knocked in the sky
As the water welled up   And washed over the buildings
The last lonely high-rise   At last licked away
And I stood in a sodden   Side street of the city
Where shades flittered blindly   With fish-flicked skull sockets
While bright overhead   An upswelling spectrum
Was lifting the living   The arc of the ark
As it rode up the water   But I came here ready
To rest where the river will rise

YAKETY HEX

KT Wagner

KT Wagner writes speculative fiction and op/ed pieces in the garden of her Maple Ridge home. She helps create and organize literary communities, including write-ins, an annual ghost-story writing retreat, and Golden Ears Writers. KT graduated from Simon Fraser University's Writer's Studio in 2015. She's a member of the Horror Writers Association of America and SF Canada, and is on the Federation of BC Writers board. A number of her short stories are published in magazines, anthologies, and podcasts. KT's work has previously appeared in Pulp Literature issues 24, 29, and 39. 'Yakety Hex' was shortlisted for our 2022 Raven Short Story Contest. KT can be found at ktwagner.com and on Facebook @northernlightsgothic or Bluesky @ktwagner.bsky.social.

Yakety Hex

Everyone always remarked on how much I resembled Grandma Gertie. In a family of tall, willowy, magically powerful women, we were two short, stocky misfits. She's my only proof I wasn't accidentally switched at birth.

Our family encouraged Grandma Gertie's interest in cross-breeding carnivorous plants. It wasn't our first choice, but then again, it wasn't her first choice either. It was a compromise, a suitable — if not ideal — pastime as she settled into her crone years.

Spinning, knitting, or select activities involving a cauldron, like soap-making, would have been preferable. However, Grandma, with her potty mouth and love of the dramatic, stomped her Doc Martens and told us in graphic detail what to do with our 'alternate ideas'.

If only we'd taken our responsibilities a little more seriously. Her neighbour's Chihuahua would still be snapping at the ankles of passersby, while Grandma and I might have continued our quest to cultivate prize-winning predatory flowers.

It all started the day after the last strand of Grandma Gertie's once-black hair transmuted into solid grey. She announced at dinner, "I've settled on my dotage project. I'm going to cultivate a traditional fairy garden on the penthouse roof."

Mother's face blanched. I studied my plate and tried not to giggle. Grandma kicked me under the table and winked when I glared. Later that evening, Mother called an emergency meeting with her five daughters. My four sisters drove in from the nearby towns and villages where they'd each set up practice. As the youngest, I still lived at home. Our sprawling apartment was nice enough, and someone had to cook, clean, and keep Grandma company during the day. Grandma growled that it was adult daycare, and I laughed. I loved spending time with her.

Mother called a meeting with her daughters. Only coven leaders like Mother can authorize the use of magic, and Grandma and I in particular had to apply in writing at least two weeks in advance. We gathered at a nearby tavern.

None of the others expressed the slightest concern about sneaking around behind Grandma's back. To drown my guilt, I ordered a large red wine and, when that didn't help, a double shot of whiskey. I wondered uneasily what they said about me when I wasn't around.

Stories about fairy gardens are passed down through our matriarchal line. My sisters and I assumed they were tall tales, until Mother leaned across the pub table that night and described the one her great-aunt built.

"A disaster," she warned. "Cultivated fairies are invasive and destructive."

They sounded fascinating. I asked for more detail while trying to keep my tone and expression serious.

Mother shut me down. "Cultivating fairies would be an absolute catastrophe and expose us completely." She made eye contact with each of us in turn. Was it my imagination, or did she hold my gaze a tad longer than the rest? "This. Is. Serious. It's our responsibility to dissuade Grandma Gertie."

While trying to picture Grandma's reaction, I almost snorted my drink out my nose. "Good luck," I managed to splutter.

Grandma always warned me I needed to learn when to be quiet — Mother and my sisters assigned negotiations to me. Above all, I was to ensure Grandma didn't use magic.

"Perhaps it will teach you something. I despair of you ever fitting in." Mother dismissed me with a wave of her hand.

I tried talking to Grandma, but she threatened to turn my hair into snakes. In the end, I was forced to cast a wee spell while crossing my fingers that Mother wouldn't find out. I had to do something.

My little intervention meant Grandma no longer coveted fairies, but she remained fixated on creating a large and impressive garden. I'd done a bit of research, but nothing I presented caught her interest until I mentioned carnivorous plants.

Soon we'd collected an impressive array of meat-eating plants. We lined a dozen kiddie pools with garbage bags, filled them with water and buckets of soil, and created muddy, bog-like homes for our new charges. I've always loved a good obsession.

Mother's fears turned from fairy invasions to the threat of her roof collapsing. Without telling me or Grandma, she purchased a tiny cottage with a garden in a retirement village not far from the loft apartment.

Grandma was thrilled. I was devastated. I didn't want Grandma to move out, and cried while she packed her suitcases. She smiled, patted my hand, told me to grow up, and said I could visit anytime.

At first, Grandma settled into her new home quite well.

Her next-door neighbour, Roland, was a pompous old geezer who wore a beret. For one hour a day, he stood on his back porch and practised his saxophone. Grandma huffed about the noise — it really was terrible — but whenever he played, she invariably wandered outside to deadhead hanging baskets, refill bird feeders, and flutter her eyelashes.

She grumbled about the man constantly while compulsively checking her hair in all reflective surfaces. Mirrors, windowpanes, and the toaster. It was nauseating.

His yappy Chihuahua wasn't impressed, and neither was Hilda, the old lady across the street. Hilda grew competition-winning roses and had her eye on another prize: Roland. For his part, Roland's pudgy face was transformed by a dimpled smile every time he caught sight of Grandma.

Grandma could barely contain her glee and set about making enemies with Hilda. "It's so much more fun than having that boring woman over for tea," she cackled.

I cackled along with her.

Grandma Gertie's competitive streak was activated. Hilda was the president of the local gardening club, so naturally Grandma joined. I went along to keep her company, and — at Grandma's urging — I proposed the 'most interesting' plant category for the annual fair. Observing Hilda seethe was great entertainment.

Afterwards, Grandma and I indulged in a glass-clinking toast in the kitchen of her cottage. We polished off the bottle while plotting our next move.

Grandma opened the door to my knock and handed me a shovel. "Right. Let's bog out that front lawn." She grinned, flashing dentures; she'd blackened one front tooth with a Sharpie. "Hilda's hissy fit will be epic. She thinks prissy little tea roses are the bee's knees."

We'd planted our carnivorous lovelies in plastic kiddie pools in the back garden, but they really needed a permanent home. I took the shovel and imagined how Mother would react if I blacked out one of my teeth with a Sharpie. I enjoyed imagining it. She certainly never showed any appreciation for my efforts to live up to her standards.

Two hours later, Hilda stood in the middle of the road, hands on hips, staring us down. "Did the homeowner's association give you permission to deface your lawn? I'm sure there's a bylaw against this."

Toward noon, Roland appeared on his porch with his saxophone. Grandma was crouched down next to the boxwood hedge, complaining about how the leaves smelled like cat piss. She straightened just in time to catch Roland dimple-smiling at Hilda.

The air shivered, and Hilda, upon observing Grandma's expression, squeaked, "Oh, my. I think I smell rain."

I hadn't realized Hilda could run that fast.

Grandma turned her charm on full and advanced on Roland. He appeared a little dazed as he lowered his lips to the mouthpiece. Then things got out of control.

The wild notes of 'Yakety Sax' filled the street—Grandma was a huge fan of old *Benny Hill Show* reruns. Hilda reappeared, rushing around like a cartoon character on fast forward, her expression a rictus of terror.

"Grandma?" I touched her shoulder. "Grandma, do you think this is a good idea? The other residents are coming outside to watch."

Grandma Gertie's eyes blazed, and she licked her lips. I grabbed both of her arms and shook. "Stop it. Mother will find out."

She stopped, but the feral expression on her face worried me.

If, originally, Grandma had been enemies with Hilda for fun, it was now a serious war. My worry grew, but I wasn't about to rat Grandma out to Mother. Besides, Mother would find a way to blame me.

I helped Grandma finish the bog gardens, and we carefully planted carnivorous bromeliads, pitcher plants, sundews, dewy pines, and Venus flytraps—Grandma tittered over that name.

She fretted over how slow the plants were to establish. One day, I arrived to find they'd all doubled in size overnight. She swore she hadn't used magic. "It was just a little extra fertilizer."

I began staying over most nights.

Hilda and Roland both appeared to be avoiding Grandma. I made a point of speaking with Roland and convinced him to come by for tea. Grandma dressed in her most colourful skirts and scarves and braided several geranium blossoms into her hair. They were pungent, but Roland didn't seem to notice. By the end of his third cup of tea and fourth homemade scone—I may not like baking, but I'm good at it—he was laughing.

The visit perked up Grandma, but not in the way I'd intended; it renewed her drive to win the garden competition. She began crossbreeding plants in the tiny garden shed. When I went to check on her, I found the door warded.

"Grandma, you know you aren't supposed to be using magic." I did my best to imitate Mother's stern tone, but my heart wasn't in it and Grandma knew it.

The chocolate-scented carnivorous cosmos was her pride and joy. It had a place of honour in a large pot on the south side of the shed and grew a foot a day. Beautiful and creepy, the cosmos was a fine specimen, but ravenous. At night, Grandma fed it squirrels. "Nasty critters. They keep stealing my birdseed."

Grandma loved to show the cosmos off to Roland. I had an uneasy feeling, but I pushed it aside, instead worrying about Mother or one of my sisters dropping by unexpectedly. They had busy, important lives and seldom even called, but it would be just my luck.

One week before the fair, Roland dropped by at the end of his daily walk, Chihuahua in tow. He was about to inhale the chocolate scent of the gigantic burgundy flowers when Hilda called from across the street, "Yoo-hoo, Roland." He turned toward Hilda, and the dog snapped at the cosmos.

My kitchen chair clattered to the floor as I leapt to my feet, but I couldn't move fast enough. Roland waved at Hilda and took a step forward. At a truncated yelp, he turned just in time to see his dog disappear down the throat of the nearest blossom.

With a dazed-looking Roland at her side, Hilda rallied the neighbours. She stood atop a turned-over plastic recycling bin and accused Grandma of all kinds of heinous behaviour.

I cast about for something to disperse the crowd. Spell-making is not a talent I've had much chance to develop. At best, I can manage small magics if I concentrate, and the scene of chaos outside of Grandma Gertie's cottage was well beyond my limited abilities.

Grandma seemed uninclined to fix the situation. In fact, I'm pretty sure she was about to curse Hilda when I slapped her hand down and pushed her back inside. Behind us, Hilda started ranting about witchcraft, and Grandma stuck her head back out the door and threatened to hex her.

I had no choice. I called Mother.

By the time Mother and my sisters arrived, the old folk of the village were practically holding torches and brandishing pitchforks.

Through an open window, Grandma taunted them. "Bring it on, bitches."

My sisters pulled her inside. Grandma raised a hand toward Mother, but never finished the motion. Mother snapped her fingers, and Grandma disappeared. I was impressed. I'd always wanted to be able to cast dramatic spells.

"She'll be back in a few minutes, right?" I held my breath.

Mother shook her head. I begged and pleaded, but Mother was adamant. Grandma couldn't be trusted. She had to be dealt with.

Eventually, I gathered myself and proposed a slight compromise. Mother agreed.

My sisters dressed me up in Grandma Gertie's clothes and added a large bonnet to conceal my dark hair. They even blacked out one of my front teeth with a Sharpie. I enjoyed that part for about five seconds before I reminded myself of the reason for it.

In full view of everyone in the retirement village, they bundled me into my eldest sister's black car and set a large canvas bag gently into the trunk.

I opened the car window a crack and listened to Mother explain to the crowd that Grandma needed to be in a hospital. She sounded like she was crying, but Mother doesn't cry. She told them Grandma had suffered a stroke and it would take too long to wait for an ambulance.

The funeral home was highly recommended by my second-eldest sister's mother-in-law, and the service was beautiful.

Roland attended and, with a little spelled help from my middle sister, played a moving rendition of 'Careless Whisper' on his saxophone.

Even Hilda showed up, but I turned her back at the door. I'd practised a small curse just for her, and it likely took days before the itching subsided.

My immediate family all shook the officiant's hand on the way out, each of us slipping him a few dollars of appreciation along with tiny everything-is-normal charms.

The roof garden is coming along, albeit on a smaller scale than before. We moved a few of Grandma's less ravenous carnivorous creations here, and they're thriving. Gardening has been added to my list of duties.

Gertie, the toad, appears comfortable. I spend time with her every day and make sure her every need is met, but I sense she's lonely. A couple of fairy friends would be a good idea once the plants have grown a little more. I no longer much care what Mother and my sisters think, and I've learned a few tricks from Grandma. "Mother doesn't need to know," I muse.

Gertie croaks in agreement.

TIMELAPSE; OR, REASONS TO PAUSE

Laura Vogt

Laura Vogt *writes historical fiction, speculative fiction, and poetry. Her poems are published in various journals, and her novelette, Blue Beyond the Sea, is available as a chapbook from Bottlecap Press. Her forthcoming debut novel, In the Great Quiet, is a historical fiction and fabulism blend based on her ancestor. She attended the University of Iowa Writers' Workshop writing program in Dublin, Ireland, and is represented by Catherine Cho of Paper Literary. Connect with her on Instagram, Goodreads, or through her website, lauravogt.com.*

Timelapse; or, Reasons to Pause

Bubbles, iridescent globes, hues of lavender,
bluebonnet, rose. Damp air, pressed breath, the

puttering of wet socks. Birdsong, your tiny ribcage,
why are the snowdrops wilting? Some say time

moves swiftly, I see it go. Barren branch to bud,
a bright yellow chicory sprouting up through the soil

in the night, smear of sleepy terrains through the car
window, what would starlight do if no one breathed

it in? Coffee spilt on pages, bubbles caught in the
plants, let's go on another adventure, but really, this

moment is perfect. This breath, that smell, the cicadas
back again, bubbles popping on my knuckle, wet

as I write. Fast, slow, not sure how to hold on, pause,
unravel, sleep for a year, I really just love the sound of

the windchimes with the roaring wind and the scent
of petrichor. Mud, air, time, skin: reasons to pause.

DOWN ALLIGATOR ALLEY

Bridget Boland

Bridget Boland's writing has appeared in Hypertext, The New Guard, Women's Sports and Fitness, YogaChicago, and The Essential Chicago. *Her debut novel,* The Doula, *was published by Simon and Schuster in September 2012. Through Modern Muse for Writers, Bridget teaches writing classes on fiction and memoir, coaches writers in creative nonfiction, fiction, and business writing, and offers seminars on yoga, energetic medicine, and writing as life-process tools. She is also a shaman and an attorney. Learn more about Bridget and her work at modernmuseforwriters.com.*

$\mathcal{D}$OWN ALLIGATOR ALLEY

They were halfway back to Naples from Miami, driving west toward the gulf side of the state on a lonely road through the Everglades, when Victor spied something ahead. He squinted into the glare of the setting sun, moved his foot to the brake, and released the cruise control.

"What the hell?" he swore under his breath as the Cadillac decelerated. He shot a quick glance at Phyllis resting beside him. Her eyes flew open in alarm.

"What is it?" His wife's tone sounded weary. *Elderly.* Her chest heaved, and she launched into a coughing fit. Victor's guts tightened. Phyllis's respiratory infections often left her bedridden or in need of oxygen. She'd just come off another round of steroids yesterday.

He shook his head and kept on, riding the brake as they approached the object. It wasn't a fallen tree trunk, as he'd guessed when they were still too far away to make it out clearly. It was an alligator. Bigger than any he'd ever seen. The beast stretched the entire width of the two-lane roadway.

As an alternative to Interstate 75, which they'd driven to Miami that morning, the GPS had offered Route 41 home through Big Cypress National Preserve. Victor had selected it on a whim. He liked road trips and exploring new terrain.

Now he regretted his impulsive choice. The narrow strip of asphalt, barely wide enough to accommodate two cars, was the only solid thing in the swampland, which stretched around them for miles. They were surrounded by water, tall grasses, and mournful cypress trees.

The car came to a stop. Victor lowered the volume on Frank Sinatra, crooning from the golden oldies station. "Sonofabitch reptile blocking my road." Victor put the car in park and slammed his hand on the horn three times. The blasting noise startled Phyllis but didn't seem to faze the gator. *Goddamned animal!* Victor slapped his palm dead centre on the horn, kept it there a good while. The blaring was loud enough to wake the dead.

Victor waited for the prehistoric-looking creature to slither off into the water that rose nearly to the edges of the road on both sides. But it didn't stir. Victor growled, tapped the horn again. He peered through the windshield, willing the animal to lash its massive tail or shift one of the small legs protruding from beneath its thick trunk. Anything to show that it could move.

Nothing.

He couldn't tell if it was alive or not.

Victor's hands dropped into his lap. He fought back a flicker of panic. His tolerance for struggle had been sorely tested in the last few years. Life seemed to have faded somehow. He could blame it on the godawful pandemic but in truth it had started before Covid. He found it more and more difficult to get excited about anything. He missed the tantalizing, ferocious desire he could still remember but never really *felt* anymore — for sex especially, but also for the heat of the sun on the beach, the refreshing chill when he waded into the ocean to cool off, the satisfaction of landing a shot on the golf course.

He took consolation in still being able to taste the oak and caramel of the Maker's Mark he drank daily before dinner. When that pleasure left him, he might as well be six feet under.

Today had brought more difficulty. When Florida announced snowbirds were eligible for the Covid vaccine, he'd signed them up online, even though it meant a two-hour drive to Miami. They'd arrived in plenty of time for their three o'clock appointment at the Dolphins' stadium, but the nurse at check-in didn't have them on her list.

"You might say we're between a rock and a hard place here at Hard Rock Stadium. My wife has a lung disease. We've driven clear across the state to get these shots." Victor had met the nurse's sceptical glare with a wink and a smile. He'd turned eighty last birthday. He was a good twenty pounds overweight, and the salt had overrun the pepper in his hair a decade ago. But he still usually won women over when he turned on the charm.

Nurse Ratched hadn't fallen for it. She'd scowled and shaken her head. "Like I've told everybody else, don't bother coming until you've gone to the state website and secured an appointment. You'll need the confirmation email, and I've got to see your names on my list."

The nurse's eyes were steely. As an attorney, Victor had spent nearly fifty years arguing for a living. Once he might have raised holy hell, but the fight had gone out of him. He and Phyllis had walked docilely back to the Cadillac. They'd made the best of the foiled trip by stopping for an early dinner. This had set them back a couple of hours, but it wouldn't have been a problem if they'd taken 75 home.

Instead, here they were, stuck in the middle of a swamp. The sun plunged beneath the horizon, and shadows gathered into darkness. There were no lights along the roadway. Nor were there any houses or other buildings. Just the never-ending wetlands. Soon it was going to be black as pitch.

Christ. Victor attempted to squelch the unease gnawing at him. A little backwater darkness was far less dangerous than all the years he'd spent navigating heavy traffic on the Dan Ryan back in the city.

But there was the gator to contend with.

He considered driving back to Miami. They could spend the night in a hotel, take their time getting back tomorrow—on 75, not this godforsaken ribbon of concrete. But his night vision wasn't what it used to be. His reaction time had slowed too, if he was honest about it. The roadway was narrow, with no margin for error. Given the way his day had gone, he'd back the car off the road into the water. He didn't dare test his luck.

Another event that had called for courage sprang to mind. Fifty years before, he'd been young and strong. Full of unearned confidence and eager for any opportunity to prove himself.

He and Phyllis were returning home late from a holiday party. Their daughter Serena, an infant, was in her car seat in the back of the Oldsmobile wagon. Victor was about to throw the change into the receptacle at the tollbooth when he noticed a state sheriff's car pulled over on the shoulder.

Next to the cruiser stood a police officer with a prisoner in a grey jumpsuit whose hands were cuffed in front of his waist. Victor's whole body tightened now as he recalled the prisoner lunging at the sheriff and yanking the officer's pistol from its holster. The officer cried out as he tried to wrestle the gun from the prisoner's hands. Driven by adrenaline-fuelled instinct, Victor had leapt from the car. He bounded over to where the prisoner was taking aim at the sheriff's chest. Victor circled wide, came up on the prisoner from behind, and tackled him to the ground. The gun discharged as it hit the pavement.

Recalling that night, Victor again felt the sharp *bang!* reverberate through him. The sheriff's office had sent him a medal and a letter calling him a hero for saving the sheriff's life. The paper had made a big to-do.

Phyllis hadn't seen it that way, though. As he started driving again, she sat white-lipped, clenching her jaw and silently sobbing.

"You could have died and left me a widow — and your child fatherless!" Phyllis had screeched when he'd asked her what was wrong.

To Victor's mind, he'd had no choice. If he'd turned a blind eye and driven on, he wouldn't have been able to live with himself. But Phyllis couldn't understand that. She'd taken Serena and moved in with her parents. They'd been separated for a year.

Staring at the gator, Victor summoned some of that virile potency of his youth. Surely it was still there, lurking in the marrow of his bones. It was weakened by age, his increasingly sedentary ways, and his poor diet, but it had been waiting for something like this: a challenge worthy of calling it forth.

"Vic?" Phyllis's voice wobbled. Her mouth bunched into a prim, worried pout. She started to say something else, but a barrage of coughs left her reaching for the inhaler she kept close at hand. The miniature silver canister hissed as Phyllis depressed the top. A sweet-scented mist filled the car. After fifty-two years of marriage, the aroma was a familiar perfume Victor associated with his wife.

"It's okay, Phyl." He filled his voice with false confidence. Phyllis continued to cough. The hacking finally abated, replaced by high-pitched wheezing every time Phyllis exhaled. Victor's pulse jumped. They hadn't brought any oxygen along. What if she had a bad attack out here?

He reached for his cell phone. He'd put Phyllis on with Serena while he figured out what to do. No service. He cursed to himself and fought back an urge to toss the damn phone into the water.

Instead, he rose out of the sedan with an involuntary groan as his lower back protested after the long ride. Then he reached back into the car and pulled a half-full plastic water bottle out of the cup holder. When he straightened up again, his XXL Jimmy Buffett T-shirt rode up from his denim shorts, exposing his gut. He yanked the cotton fabric down and stomped toward the gator.

He'd left the car door open. The insistent chime echoed like a recrimination. It fed his ire, which flared along with his sciatica.

Halfway to the behemoth, he paused. The asphalt beneath his feet felt spongy. He looked at the water surrounding him, its inky blackness reflecting the black night sky. Suddenly it seemed foolhardy—arrogant, actually—to attempt to traverse an untamed landscape on a thin layer of asphalt that had no business cutting through a swamp. But here he was. He had to do something to get them out of this mess. Victor stepped back with his right foot, cocked the water bottle over his shoulder, and flung it at the beast. The bottle struck its jagged back with a dull thud, ricocheted off, tumbled to the roadway, and rolled into the water.

The goddamned gator didn't move. Victor huffed, frustration prickling hot up his neck, into his face. He looked around for something else to toss at the animal, but the roadway was empty of debris.

He moved nearer, squinting at the form hulking in the darkness. He swore softly, lifted the Cubs hat from his head, wiped sweat from his brow, replaced the cap. His intestines grumbled, along with his lower back.

He cursed his stupidity, spun around, and rushed to the Cadillac. The interior light was on, a spotlight on the raw panic on Phyllis's face. Victor reached in and switched on the headlights.

The headlamps shone on the midsection of the gator. Scales rose like mountain peaks along its massive body, which was three feet or more across. Thick, calcified nails on each foot gleamed in the glare of the twin beams.

Victor traced the form to the right, his eyes needing a moment to adjust as they travelled past the reach of the headlamps down the length of the tail. It disappeared into the water. Then he scanned the creature until he located the vague form of the gator's head far beyond the glow of the lights, clear at the other end of the two-lane roadway.

Goddamnit.

Victor emitted a martyr's sigh. He'd have to reposition the car. He plunked back down into the driver's seat, started the Cadillac, put it into reverse, and backed up several feet. He yanked the steering wheel hard to the left until the headlights shone onto the creature's front end. Phyllis gasped and grabbed for her door handle.

The head was tilted at a cockamamie angle that made Victor shiver. The animal might very well be dead after all. He'd have to get closer.

Victor struggled out of the car. The air was humid and still. He inched closer, stopping about ten feet shy of the beast. *Sonofabitch.* Even if the creature was dead, it was too large for him to push or shove or lift out of his path.

He looked over his shoulder at Phyllis, who was taking another pull off her inhaler. He turned back to the beast and stepped close enough to inspect the eye on the side facing him. A filmy residue covered the pupil like a cataract. Surely that meant the creature was dead.

But what if it wasn't? What if he tried to get it to move and it attacked? His insides trembled at the notion of that mighty tail sweeping him off his feet, the immense jaws clamping down on his torso. He widened his stance to steady himself as he peered at the creature, which gave no sign that it registered Victor's presence.

A shrill scream cut the night. It sliced through Victor too, skittering up and down his spine. The sound hadn't come from the gator. He backed away from it anyway, his head turning wildly as he sought the source of the shrieking. He thought it was Phyllis. But though his wife had her head in her hands, she wasn't making any sound.

Another hair-raising screech filled Victor's ears. Adrenaline lit through him. The screaming made the night ominously alive, as if the darkness were a living, breathing creature that was about to swallow him and Phyllis — the Cadillac, even — whole, leaving behind no trace of their existence.

Recently he and his grandson Arlo had watched some survival show about the Everglades. The narrator had spoken of jaguars that lived in the swamps. In a dramatic tone, he'd described them as sixty pounds of sleek ebony muscle, nocturnal creatures that stalked the night looking for prey.

Did big cats swim? Victor wracked his brain to remember what all the narrator had said. He consoled himself with the thought that sound carried over water. Perhaps the cat was a long way off.

Or maybe the gator really was dead, and the cat's keen sense of smell had picked up on the carcass sitting out here.

The night went still again. Victor took a breath. He turned his attention back to the giant reptile. How the hell was he going to find out for sure if it was dead or alive?

He had half a sawed-off broom handle in the car. After reading about post-Covid looting in the South, he'd put it in the Cadillac for the long ride from Chicago to Florida. He wasn't comfortable carrying a pistol; he wasn't certain he'd be able to use one if it came to that. But with the broom handle, he could threaten a blow to the head if someone underestimated him and tried any funny business.

He rushed back to the car and felt around on the floor of the back seat until he located the broom handle.

"Please be careful!" Phyllis pleaded as he drew it out and hurried back to the gator.

He jutted his right arm out and jabbed the beast in the side with the blunt end of the broom handle.

The gator didn't move.

Victor jabbed it again. And again. "Jah! Jah!" he hollered the third time, hoping that the urgent call, coupled with the poking, would incite movement.

His daughter Serena was part of that animal rights group. Were gators on the endangered species list? He couldn't recall. No matter. The PETA people would flay him alive if they could see him.

Victor glared at the gator, willing it to move. Not a single flicker. He blew out a breath of defeat, certain now that it was dead. The last of his hope evaporated. No way could he push, pull, or drag a half-ton corpse off the roadway.

But if it *was* dead, could he drive right over the monster?

He shut his eyes. He imagined backing up the Cadillac to build momentum and speed and then launching the sedan at the beast.

He shook his head. He would either strike the animal and flip the Cadillac or drive over it slowly and get stuck halfway. Then he would be well and truly screwed.

He and Phyllis could climb over it. Phyllis would have fits, but he could bully her into it if it came to that. But being on the other side without the car wasn't going to help. He recalled the scream that had cut through him earlier.

His blood pressure skyrocketed as he dismissed all the ways he could think of to get them out of this mess.

Finally, he threw his head back and roared. Fear and caution swept away by his irate fury, he charged the alligator, the broom handle raised overhead. He rained blows down on the creature's leathery hide.

The beast gave no response. Phyllis called out to him, but Victor ignored her. Infuriated, he swung again and again, jabbing its sides, beating its back. He cried out in anguished frustration. He was furious—with the beast, the goddamned nurse who'd turned them away, the virus, Phyllis's illness, old age.

Everything seemed to be conspiring against him, nudging him closer and closer to the moment, somewhere in a future that felt all too near at hand, when he held his last breath and evaporated into what he felt certain was a darkness as complete and immense as the one he was standing in.

His chest grew tight, and his heart pounded a sharp warning. Still, Victor howled like some contemporary Captain Ahab, his white whale a colossal lizard.

It figured that a kid like him, who'd come up from the blue-collar neighbourhoods of Chicago, would find his nemesis not in the worthy adversary of a leviathan but in a gritty, amphibious sewer dweller. His law partners and golf buddies would have a field day if he met his end facing down a damn dead reptile. There was no dignity to be had in a death like that.

Victor's stubbornness had seen him through many a hard time. Now Life was conspiring against him, luring him into this dilemma he couldn't get out of no matter how hard he tried.

His next thought sank his spirits entirely.

Life wasn't out to get him. Death was.

Awareness struck hard, swift as a kick to the gut: he wasn't getting out of this life alive. No one did. Sure, he and Phyllis might find their way out of the Everglades. They had the car, and while the night would be long, it wouldn't go on forever. But neither would his life …

Fuelled by impotent rage, futility, and, underneath those, existential terror, Victor raised the pole again and whacked the gator. He gasped as his heart clutched, sending shooting pain through his chest.

He kept at it until the anger ran out of him. Exhaustion set in. His T-shirt dripped with sweat. His arms quivered long after he stopped swinging the pole. His hands went slack.

The pole clattered onto the pavement and rolled into the water. The broom handle sank under the surface.

Victor sobbed. Rage had turned into something as near to grief as he dared go. He wasn't an insensitive man, but he'd learned long ago to keep a tight lid on his feelings. Still, he felt weary to the bone. He seemed so small in comparison to the gator, the endless darkness of the water, and the skies.

Victor doubled over and propped his hands on his knees. He recalled Serena reading a poem at his brother's graveside. *Do not go gentle into that good night. Rage, rage, against the dying of the light.*

Yes, he had thought as they'd lowered Richard, who had been far more mild-mannered, into the ground. *I will go down kicking and screaming. I'll fight for every single goddamn extra second I can get.*

Now he feared he'd been mistaken. Arrogant. He *wasn't* a young buck of thirty anymore; the kid who'd thought himself unstoppable, immortal. The one who'd leapt on that prisoner, eager for the opportunity to prove his bravery and strength.

He was goddamned lucky to have survived these eighty years. To have outlived not just his parents but also his younger sibling. As much as Richard's death had pained him, he'd also felt an unexpected swell of pride at being the last man standing.

Staring out into the blackness, he felt bereft, his body heavy. Victor's knees buckled. He thought about lying down right there under the sky. Perhaps there was a grace in surrendering to the infinite darkness. He could count stars until he lost track of himself, fell asleep, maybe even rolled off into the water.

He had begun to sink to the pavement in utter capitulation when Phyllis, bathed in the light inside the car, caught his eye. The night with the sheriff rose in Victor's mind again. Phyllis had resented his decision, as if he'd rejected her and their marriage by helping the cop. Now her eyes locked on his, silently beseeching him to do something.

He couldn't save them. There was no way to do that. But he could do what he hadn't been able to the night he'd helped the sheriff. He could comfort Phyllis. Let her know he was there with her and that he wasn't going anywhere.

The sight of his wife in the car was so inviting. His back and his knees protesting, Victor drew himself up to his full height, walked back to the car, and dropped down into the driver's seat.

Phyllis's eyes widened when he slipped his arm around her. For a few moments she felt brittle in his embrace, as if she was steeling herself for more catastrophe. Victor leaned in and pressed his lips on hers reverently, with all the gratitude and affection he felt for his wife but didn't often show. She gave him a wan smile, put her head on his shoulder, and settled into his embrace. She seemed at ease now. As if she had made her own peace with the inevitable end they never spoke of drawing nearer.

Victor yawned. He shut his eyes. A soft breeze skipped in through the open windows. He pushed the radio button. On came Ol' Blue Eyes, crooning about strangers in the night.

Phyllis gave a small cry of delight. It was the song they'd danced to at their wedding.

They were far from strangers. For the first time since he'd stopped the car, Victor felt glad just to be there, alone in the enveloping darkness with his wife.

THE BUMBLEBEE FLASH FICTION CONTEST

THE 2024 BUMBLEBEE FLASH FICTION CONTEST

This year's Bumblebee Flash Fiction Contest presented us with a colony of delightful entries. Of our shortlist, this is what final judge Bob Thurber had to say: *"It is always a joyful experience to judge the Bumblebee Contest. Again this year, I'm honoured by the opportunity and wonderstruck by the fine batch of offerings with a variety of themes."*

Winner: 'The Scientific Method' by Alan Sincic
Honourable Mentions: 'All but Pink' by Megan W Shaw, 'Girl of My Dreams' by Jodi MacAulay, and 'Managing a Difficult Situation With Grace' by Leslie Wibberley

The winning story ultimately captured Bob's attention with *"its quirky aesthetic and obvious merit."* He also offered *"enthusiastic nods"* to the unranked honourable mentions, saying, *"My heartfelt congratulations to all the finalists. Nice work. You should be proud."*

Congratulations to all of the shortlisted authors:

Alan Sincic	Malumir R Logan
Cat Girczyc	Marta Anielska
Dianne Kenny	Megan W Shaw
Jodi MacAulay	Neil Jefferies
Leslie Wibberley	Scott MacLeod

A teacher at Valencia College, **Alan Sincic** *has published fiction in* The Saturday Evening Post, Boulevard Online, New Ohio Review, The Greensboro Review, *and elsewhere. His short stories have recently won contests sponsored by* Press 53, The Texas Observer, Driftwood Press, *and others. And two have previously appeared in* Pulp Literature, *in issues 31 and 37. After receiving an MA in Literature at the University of Florida and a poetry fellowship at Columbia, he earned his MFA at Western New England University. A native Floridian, he spent more than a dozen years in NYC as a writer and performer of comic/satirical pieces that eventually became a pair of full-length plays (*American Obsessions *and* Breaking Glass*). Visit him at alansincic.com.*

Jodi MacAulay *is an emerging writer living in Calgary. She is a member of the Writers' Guild of Alberta and the Alexandra Writers' Centre Society. She is a contributor to the Friday Flash Fiction website and is currently working on a short story collection inspired by her small-town roots in the Canadian Rockies.*

Leslie Wibberley *lives in a suburb of Vancouver, Canada, with her amazing family and an overly enthusiastic cocker spaniel. Her work is published in multiple literary journals and anthologies, including the Bram Stoker-nominated* Not All Monsters *and the Aurora-nominated* Prairie Witch. *Her stories have placed first in the* Writer's Digest Annual Writing Competition *and* Popular Fiction Awards. *She is represented by Naomi Davis of Bookends Literary. Leslie's work has appeared in* Pulp Literature *twice before: 'Stonecold' (winner of Creative Ink's Flash Fiction Contest) in Issue 21 and 'Attempted Murder' in Issue 32. Visit her at lesliewibberley.com.*

Megan W Shaw *is a writer and a secondary school teacher for the Toronto District School Board. Her fiction appears in* Cossmass Infinities, The Arcanist, *and* Polar Borealis. *Her story 'The Realm of Shadows' appeared in* Pulp Literature *Issue 34, Spring 2022. 'All but Pink' was an honourable mention in the 2024 Bumblebee Flash Fiction Contest.*

The Scientific Method

by Alan Sincic

Long before I read the book about how the father and the mother collide — the diagram of the docking manoeuvre and the pics all prickly with arrows pointing to the tumbler and the spring and the shank — I'd assembled a picture of my own.

You begin with a bun. Bun in the oven. Baby out the body of the mother. But by the time I was ten or so, I knew you need a kind of yeast to make it — the bread, the baby — rise. But where do you get the yeast? Where does it come from? In *National Geographic* I read about a sponge in the sea, stuck to a rock or whatever, and it releases, like a sneeze, a batch of little spores, a cloud of spores to random off into the open ocean to meet, eventually, the mother sponge.

The air is an ocean, right? The one thing we all of us share. The one thing we — every single minute — swallow into the centre of the self. And particles. You got particles in the air. Smoke. Clouds. And through the air they travel, and from one person to another. Billions of particles you vacuum into that hollow in the heart of you.

So over the course of a season I cobbled together a theory. I could see in the neighbour kids, how in the shape of the face or the cut of the frame or the hitch of the step they carried the echo of the mother and the father both, the two together under the same roof, as if the nearness was a key, as if the rafters and the beams, the counter and the bookshelf, and the high top of the dresser captured the spores of the father as he, day after day, exfoliated hither and thither. It was everywhere, the dust. Dust with a direction. A stir in the air. The mother breathes. Ignition.

So there you go. A breath of air becomes, in the end, a baby. And even after I found, at the end of the summer, at a rummage sale in the basement of the Presbyterian church, the recipe itself, the blueprint, a hardback no bigger than a book of prayer, the binding in a ripple and the glossy paper swollen with the stains of a flood or a leak or a storm—*The Matrimonial Bond: Advice For Newlyweds*—and pried it apart, shucked it like an oyster to find inside it the shock of a lifetime, I clung to the original theory. You can talk all you want about the plumbing, the innards all icky with a liquidy goo, the bang-bang-bang of the bodies, but no. Gimme the air. The breath of air. Something majestic about air. Big enough to buoy a moon. Small enough to cinder a cigar. The breath of God, right?

PULP Literature

The Bumblebee
Flash Fiction Contest
Deadline: 15 February
Prize $300

The Magpie Award for Poetry
Deadline: 15 April
Prize $500

The Hummingbird Flash Fiction Prize
Deadline: 15 June
Prize $300

The Raven Short Story Contest
Deadline: 15 October
Prize $300

The Kingfisher Poetry Prize
Deadline: 15 November
Prize $300

Enter today:
pulpliterature.com/contests

Girl of My Dreams

by Jodi MacAulay

I don't polish the furniture much anymore. I hardly ever mop the floor, either. I've always preferred gardening, so the cat determines the housekeeping schedule. When he starts playing with dust bunnies under the dining table, I stay indoors and clean.

The divorce will be final soon. What a relief. Who would have thought twenty-five years of love and trust could end like an untied balloon, blatting around overhead in a manic circle before shrivelling to the floor?

When my husband left, he shouted, "There is no Ice Capades."

It's true. The company went bankrupt back in the nineties. The general public didn't want to see Las Vegas—style chorus girls on skates anymore.

But I did. That's all I ever wanted.

When I was little, my dream was to be an Ice Capette—a member of the precision team in the ice show. Being a soloist was out of the question. My family couldn't afford skating lessons. There was no one to teach me to hop, jump, or spin, so I taught myself to glide, stop, and turn. An Ice Capette's job was to keep her line straight. To kick. To smile. I knew I could do it if I got the chance.

And the costumes. Oh, the costumes. Ice Capettes wore spangled confections cut high at the thigh, with fishnet tights stretching down their legs. They put covers over their skates to match their outfits, but the headpieces were my favourite. Sometimes they had feathers, sometimes sparkles. They elevated the Ice Capettes from a cluster of hometown pretties to a constellation of cultivated wonder. I couldn't imagine growing up to be anything else, but by the time I was old enough for a tryout, Ice Capades was taking its final bow.

Where does a dream go when it cannot die? It sinks deeper into the soft place where it's always lived, where it's murmured to you for as long as you can remember. It aches, so you cradle it. You reassure it — whisper to it, promise it — *Your time will come.*

I became a bookkeeper, a wife. The world went in and out of lockdown. I looked in the mirror one morning, and my dream was staring me in the face. What was I to do? Grab that glittering girl by the shoulders and shake her? Tell her to get over it?

Then my husband left.

He was right. There is no Ice Capades. Arenas are filled by lady rock stars, solo acts wearing Versace bodysuits and Christian Louboutin boots, singing about dull things like honesty and keeping it real. No skates or pristine sheets of ice. No perfect beauties in a rotating line, turning faster and faster until the Ice Capette on the end breaks free and can't skate quick enough to catch up.

It doesn't matter if Ice Capades is gone. When you've been the whirling girl your entire life — the one who breaks free — the audience gasps, but you know it's a trick. You let go on purpose to show how fast the line is moving.

The lawn needs mowing today. I'm fussy about the yard, and doing the grass is something I'm particularly good at. I have perfected a number of cutting patterns to keep the sod healthy — simple stripes, crisp diagonals, sharp diamonds. I'll get dressed and go out, but one of my skate guards needs fixing first. The spring holding it on the blade came loose. With a little help from a screwdriver, it'll be good as new.

I'm wearing my blue costume today because I like the matching headpiece. It has feathers on it and a birdcage veil embellished with sequins and tiny seed pearls.

When I put on my skates, I stand tall. My husband said it wasn't normal to walk around like that. I told him it wasn't normal to live with regret.

He told me to get help.

What he can't understand, and what a lot of people don't know, is that skates *provide* support. The idea that certain people can't skate because they have weak ankles is a load of hooey. Any Ice Capette worth her costume will tell you there is no such thing as weak ankles.

Quality skates, with properly fitted boots, give you all the support you need.

Managing a Difficult Situation with Grace

by Leslie Wibberley

Grace rolls over, each one of her seventy-nine years making itself known in a noisy chorus of snaps and pops. Sunlight streams through the open window and dapples the floorboards. John hated to sleep with the window open, but Grace loves the whispery breezes that carry the sweet scent of roses. The delicate perfume usually prompts a smile.

But not today.

Today, she wants to scream at the unfairness of life. At fifty-five years of marriage being tossed aside like an empty Ziploc bag.

She sits up, feet dangling over the edge of the bed. Coffee. She needs coffee. Black and bitter, like her heart. She slides forward and stands, her right foot landing smack-dab in a pool of tepid urine.

Her face twists in disgust. "Randall!" This is the third mess the elderly spaniel has made this week.

Rage erupts, blazing through her like a wildfire as she hops to the bathroom. Grabbing a towel, she scrubs her foot so hard her skin tingles. "Pathetic. Can't even control your own bladder. No wonder John doesn't want you in his fancy new life."

She flings the towel away and stomps down the hallway in search of the dog. When she finds him, she's going to smoosh his face into this latest mess. Teach him a lesson.

"Randall!" she calls again. She checks every room on the top floor. He doesn't usually go downstairs before her in the mornings. Where the hell is he?

The pulse thudding at Grace's temples reminds her that, despite the new meds, her blood pressure is still too high. She forces air in through her nose and out through pursed lips for a count of four. Square breathing, designed to reduce stress and anxiety.

Doesn't do a damned thing.

Not surprising. Grace's anxiety levels have been hovering in the stratosphere since John walked out on them yesterday.

She clomps down the stairs. Age may have stripped her body down to a frail shell of its former self, but the wooden planks groan with each footfall. Anger grants heft to even the tiniest of persons.

"Randall. Here, boy. Such a good dog." Grace grits her teeth, trying to control the wrath that paints her innocuous words scarlet. Her Randall is a smart boy. He'll sense her mood. Even if he's within hearing range, he'll never come to her.

Reaching the bottom of the steps, Grace finds another puddle of urine. More proof of her dog's ageing body, and an unwelcome reminder of the inevitability of a bleak, lonely future.

Her anger softens.

Fades.

Tips over an invisible precipice into sorrow.

No longer sustained by rage, Grace's body deflates. Sighing, she skirts the mess and heads to the kitchen for a roll of paper towel.

She crouches to clean up the mess. Long past their prime, her knees complain bitterly at the awkward position. Her thigh muscles cramp, and she drops hard onto her buttocks. A starburst of pain lights up her arthritic spine. Dampness creeps across the crotch of her pyjama pants.

Not again.

She tries valiantly to ward off a wave of shame, but it comes anyway, along with a rush of tears.

She knew about John's affairs, had for years, but she chose to ignore them. In her mind, being alone was far worse than being betrayed.

But he left them anyway.

A wet nose pushes against her leg. Randall eases himself under her arm and leans against her as if to say, "I'm here, and I love you."

Grace presses a kiss to his greying forehead. "My sweet boy." She strokes his silky ears. "Give me a minute to clean up this mess and get dressed, and then we'll go for a walk."

The dog's bark is as bright and joyful as a puppy's. He licks away her tears and dances in place.

All but Pink

by Megan W Shaw

"It's the wrong colour."

"It's a nice colour?"

"Nice is not the goal." I glare at Mabel. "Pink is the goal—bright pink."

"Well, Dash, you got the bright part down. It's like I'm looking into the eyes of the Ice Witch."

Mabel's laugh sounds a bit forced, a bit cold. I regret my glare and wish I could hear her laugh as it used to be: light and pixie-like.

She turns back to her herb prep.

I stir the glacier-blue potion, trying to think of a fix. I don't want to waste this batch. Some of the ingredients were difficult to acquire.

The markers of the recipe were all correct up to this point:

INGREDIENT	METHOD	MARKER
grass of a sunny day (2 blades)	stir, two rotations	sweetgrass green
coal of a stormy night (1 piece)	drop, causing a splash	predawn purple
sweat of a lover's play (⅛ tsp)	stir, one rotation	navel orange
scream of a darling's fright (1 s)	sound over liquid	midnight blue
taste of a home-shared dish (2 0 g)	place gently, allowing to sink	whole-milk white
words of a close-shared wish (1 wish)	recite over liquid	hollyhock pink

My dear Amorine roasted a chicken for our dinner last night, and a leftover piece made the potion the perfect colour of whole milk — white and opaque, not watery at all. But the last ingredient, the words of a close-shared wish. What went wrong? This blue colour is as far from hollyhock pink as one can get.

I remove the spoon from the potion. The liquid ripples, causing a flickering effect, as if I'm commanding a blue-white star to twinkle.

There is affection between Amorine and me. I know that. Not just because I believe it, but because the markers were correct until now. The potion wouldn't turn purple without infatuation, or orange without desire; it couldn't become blue without care, or white without —

"What's your shared wish?" Mabel is leaning over my potion. She peers into it and then into my face. A sprig of thyme sticks out of the corner of her mouth.

"Uh, some space, please?"

"Sure." Mabel steps back to her prep station and tosses the thyme in the compost bin. "But really, what was your last ingredient?"

"It—" The potion continues to ripple, glimmering white and blue.

"Because that colour looks more like care and familiarity to me, not a compatible future."

Care and familiarity. Amorine is familiar with the future I want, and she cares about it, but she does not share it.

Dammit.

"Amorine doesn't want to leave Lumen Village," I blurt.

"Ah," Mabel says, understanding my wish. "That's certainly how it looks."

"Does it matter, though?" My voice startles the doves above Mabel's prep station. One beats its wings against the cage, dislodging a perfectly good feather. "If everything else lines up, isn't that enough?"

Mabel's expression sours. She's ever the moral witch.

I scowl at the potion, averting my eyes from Mabel's. I look over at her hands. They are tense and green-stained, but elegant. Her long fingers grasp a sprig of rosemary with intensity, but also without bruising the leaves.

The ripples in the potion still and the brightness fades. Any magic that was building up in the liquid has dissipated. I scowl and then breathe deeply, trying to compose myself.

"How do you know so much about this love potion?" I ask Mabel.

Mabel hesitates and looks away from me. When she looks back, her eyes are shiny. "I tried to make it once. Got stuck exactly where you did."

"Oh, I'm—"

"It's fine, Dash. It's good that it didn't work."

"Why?"

"Because it's okay to erase someone's insecurities and hesitations so that they can embrace love. It's not okay to erase the future that they want."

Mabel sticks the sprig of rosemary into her mouth as she turns away from me. The door of the laboratory shuts behind her. "Oh, Mabel." My anger fades, leaving me calm and also cold. Much like Mabel seems when she's around me.

I pick up the cauldron and pour its contents into the sink. Hours of planning and collecting swirl down the drain, breaking into the various colour markers. It's pretty, really. A rainbow whirlpool of green, purple, orange, blue. All but pink.

FASTENERS

Michaela Chan

In 'Fasteners', fathers and daughters consider giving up. What does quitting make room for? **Michaela Chan** *wrote this story on the shore of Lake Michigan as she made plans to move back to the shore of Lake Ontario. Her pages seek the sweet intersection of brevity and meaning. She is the fifth of six siblings. Visit Michaela at michaelachan.com for small stories and everyday experiences.*

Sea and Hay met before noon if they met at all. Pulling down grapevines and sumac were tasks unsuited for midday. Sea and Hay kept to their respective sides of the fence, Sea's fence. A hill spooled past, and in its indifference lost a curve. Hay's clipped property cinched Sea's.

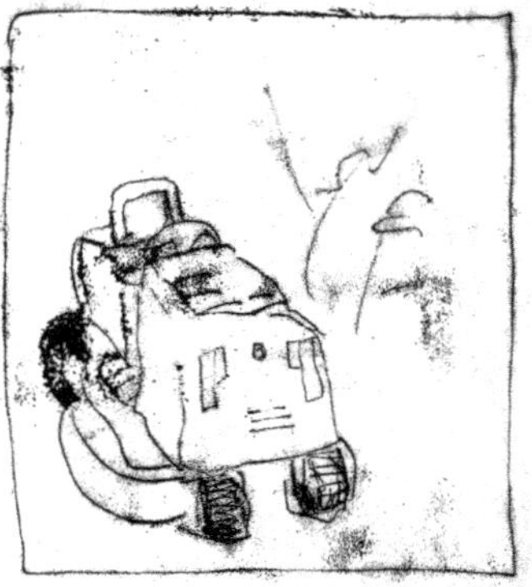

Hay knew that the tractor was new to Sea's collection. Grass had not yet sprouted, flowered, and seeded through it.

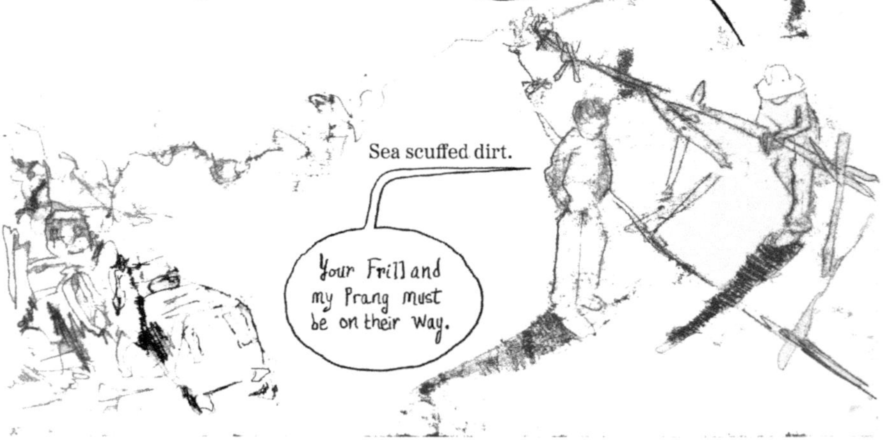

Sea scuffed dirt.

In fact, their daughters had arrived at the lake minutes ago. The smoke of charcoal grills mingled with trees. Breezy conversation. Children escaped parents laden with bags.

Prang pushed open the umbrella. A bent spoke. Frill laid out two towels, one practical and one aspirational. A boy might sit beside Frill. She tracked the boy's ball up to where gulls looped in shrieking circles.

Prang poured sand into a hole in the pole of the old umbrella.

Earlier that morning, her dad, Sea, had induced an avalanche when he pulled the umbrella out.

Frill wanted to know the
others better. Who will
lose sorely? Who will
refuse? Who will quit?

Her legs draped. She gave
her length to the boys'
line of sight.

Hay wanted
Sea to rip up
the fence.

Sea inspected a stray
blown nest. The fence
indicated a property line.
The nouveau rural did not
raise livestock or crops.

Sea had been gathering leftover paint. Poured into a drum and swirled. There was not enough paint for the whole fence yet. Hay would have to wait on a fence update.

A boy dove for the ball, kicking up a spray of sand. Prang got some in her eye.

Frill squinted at the pier. Quarter mile or so for the boy's race.

The ball rolled to Frill's toes. She passed it back. The boy added a hop in his sprint back to the game.

Will you get what you want?

Frill laughed. Most girls don't get it.

Probably.

What do you want?

I WANt to QUit thiNgs.

Why?

The umbrella is a pinwheel stamp on blue.
Why start things?
No empty space to stretch.
Obedient and pleasing.
Quit. But. I astonish myself.
I'm terrified I'm not passionate.
Too many things.
Things accumulate.

QUittiNg iS AN AccoMPLisHMeNt.

Frill was familiar with Prang's silent and invisible deep breaths. They were best friends.

Hay turned uphill.

Sea watched Hay recede. Wildflowers and singing insects did not slow his neighbor.

Funny little man, Sea. Wrecks the view with his junk heap.

Men like Hay should look a long time at trash.

Then they might quit. I might quit.

Ha Ha

TAKE MY HAND: SLEEP WITH ONE EYE OPEN

Mel Anastasiou

Mel Anastasiou writes the Fairmount Manor Mysteries, the Hertfordshire Pub Mysteries, and the Monument Studios Mysteries. Winner of a Literary Titan Gold award and longlisted for the Leacock Medal, Mel is also the author of two illustrated thirty-day workbooks on story structure: the steampunk-themed The Writer's Boon Companion and The Writer's Friend and Confidante. For news on published and upcoming works, visit her website, melanastasiou.wordpress.com.

Take My Hand
Part 2: Sleep With One Eye Open

In 'Sleep With One Eye Open,' Part 2 of Take My Hand: A Ghost Story, *it's April 1991. By day, Jamie Stewart hides out from the criminal family who adopted her. By night, she's an orderly in a city hospital——and an easy mark for a spirit intent on possessing her.*

Chapter 4

The night shift over, Jamie Stewart stood restless and undecided outside the hospital emergency entrance. In one hand she held a paper cup of coffee and in the other the straw handbag containing the pages of ghost writing. She looked for the Churleys' blue van, in case it was coming at last to take her to what the criminal family called *home*. Of course, they were just as unlikely to find her today as on any previous day. But that was statistical thinking, and Jamie didn't trust it for a moment. She did trust her careful habits. Caution said, *Go back to your apartment. Double-lock the doors. Stay hidden and sleep.* Throughout the winter she had been happy enough to comply. But now it was spring, and Japanese cherries blossomed under a bright blue sky. She wanted to walk. Like normal people who weren't hiding from crooks in daylight and ghosts at night.

She drank the last of her coffee, tossed the cup into the trash bin beside the emergency door, and walked east under the cherry trees lining the sidewalks.

A blue panel van caught her up. It approached, and she turned away to hide her face from driver and passenger until it drove off. There were many blue vans in the world, and most of them weren't after her. But she was grateful for the cherry trees' dappling shadows, which made an ever-changing disguise. As well, along with the steady stream of traffic, there were a good many pedestrians in this section of town, apartment dwellers who walked the tree-lined blocks towards school or work or took transit downtown. She felt nearly invisible among them. The apartment buildings differed in siding colours and the observable dedication of their caretakers to the lawns. Here was a vacancy sign. There, a couple manhandled a recliner through a front door. Further on, a woman stood in her window, looking down.

Jamie glanced at every car, van, and pedestrian that passed. She gripped her straw bag, with the ghost writing inside it, tight against her side. She wondered how to think rationally about the supernatural when reality was enough of a problem. Admittedly, her life in hiding was a pressure cooker, but she knew as well as she knew anything that she wasn't crazy. Poorly adjusted, certainly, and the old joke that *you're not paranoid if they're really after you* certainly applied to her. On the other hand, she was so used to being pursued that it was possible, as the months wore on and the Churleys didn't find her, that she might have invented a ghost who did. But the pages of ghost writing existed. She hadn't imagined Casey's writing. Nor her powerlessness under his control.

Once she set disbelief to one side, logic came into play. She wished her engineer mother were alive to help her with it. Or, if not alive, she wished her mother was a ghost, too. She might ask her, *if we posit for the sake of argument that Casey is real, and a ghost, then why did he choose me to write his story?*

One potential reason was that Jamie's mother was born near Saigon, and Vietnamese persons were exceptionally open to the idea of ghosts. However, Jamie's father was an American soldier, and the few memories she had of his visits to their rooms called up the square face and clever, humorous gaze of a man who thought for himself and was unlikely to accept superstitions.

If it wasn't that Jamie was half-Vietnamese, then it didn't matter whose hand he took over, and if he was real, then Casey would almost certainly choose somebody else next time.

This was a comforting conclusion at which to arrive. Jamie breathed easier and walked on past a row of duplexes, heading further east. As a child, she loved to walk, and even upon her arrival in North America from Vietnam, orphaned by pirates at sea and awaiting adoption by whatever family would take her in, she rambled for hours when permitted. But when she understood that the adoptive family were also pirates, in their way, she found an open window in their house, wiggled outside, and walked off. All walks stopped when the Churleys recaptured her — Mag Churley, in the family van, with her nephew Daino in the back to do the strong-arming. After that, Jamie left the family's home only under escort and to get schooling, since the

Churleys' favoured education. Their landlubber piracy relied upon a veneer of confidence and intelligence, and smart crooks with smart minions brought criminal success. So it was that, on her last day of junior college, Jamie had escaped alone. Not without help, but alone.

The sun was well overhead when Jamie turned a corner and entered a wide street packed with small businesses. Here, mock-Tudor façades held a slight edge over tile, plate glass and plastic brick. The only apartments were one- or two-storey units atop the shops and cafés. She slowed her pace and strolled along the shopfronts. Bead shop, women's boutique, corner convenience store.

Thank all the gods of every land, it's over.

As if on cue, her hand began to twitch.

Jamie stopped short. She rubbed her palm over the smooth new denim of her jeans. The tingling grew stronger. Or was it not more like a prickling, as if her hand had gone to sleep? But she was afraid that something was waking up.

Jamie's hand reached for—

The physical urge, separate from her will, was the same she'd failed to resist in the shadows of the hospital.

Her hand reached for—

Pen and paper were not there. Of course not. She was standing in late-afternoon sunshine on a busy sidewalk.

And she didn't have what was needed.

Her free hand clasped her twitching hand to hold it as steady as possible at the wrist. Her arms surrounded her straw bag and held it tight to her chest. People stared at her as they passed, and truly she must have been a sight, quivering on the sidewalk beside the shopfronts, one hand attempting to stop the other from reaching out.

She pushed her affected hand inside her straw bag. It stirred up the pages of computer paper it found there, communicating the ghost's eagerness to carry on writing its story. But those pages were already filled with his handwriting.

She must have paper. As well, she needed a pen.

She didn't actually want either of these items, but she had to have them.

Sweat pricked at her forehead. How could it be that all around her were shops selling every product the world of retail offered — except stationery?

To hide her misery from the flow of passers-by, she stared at the convenience shop window. It was plastered with posters advertising foodstuffs and magazines, and one of the posters was emblazoned with the neon-lettered invitation *Get your school tools here.*

Wes Gates looked up from his newspaper when the door of his family's cluttered convenience shop chimed. A young woman in jeans stepped inside. The paper kites hanging overhead swung as the door closed behind her.

Wes said, "Good morning."

The woman didn't answer. *Snob,* he thought cheerfully, and returned to the mental debate he was having with a guy in 'Letters' who was either a fool or a fascist. But he kept half an eye on the young woman as she walked up and down the short aisles, wringing her hands and apparently searching for something. She seemed distressed. So, maybe not a snob. Maybe not well. Or perhaps fragile, and about to tip mentally into something unmanageable. Like any shop clerk, he'd seen it all before. Wes folded his paper, pushed it onto a shelf beneath the cash register, and stepped out from behind the counter.

He asked the young woman, "Want help finding something?"

She turned her gaze to him and registered such distress that he asked himself whether he ought to run upstairs to his family's apartment for a mop and bucket.

Maybe she was pregnant. "Look, are you sick? You look ready to throw up."

"If I could just get some ..." She trailed off.

"Ginger ale?"

"... paper."

"Ginger ale will make you feel better. Or at least give you something sweet to throw up. We've got lots."

"I'm not sick. Please, do you have any paper?"

"Sure. We have foolscap, binder paper, and lawyer's pads." He couldn't remember when he'd last seen desperation like that in anybody's eyes. "Paper's at the end of the aisle here."

She wrapped one hand around her middle and covered it with her other hand.

Was there something wrong with her arm?

"We also carry pain relief, over here at the counter."

"No. Paper, please."

From the shelf at the end of the aisle, he picked up a yellow legal pad and handed it to her.

She took it from him with her left hand and thanked him. Her right hand was doing something strange, and he stared at the slim fingers that appeared to be writing words in the air. She captured her right hand with her left and pinned it against her stomach along with the legal pad.

She said, "And a pen. Please."

Wes handed her a ballpoint from a display on the register counter.

Her right hand escaped the legal pad and seized the pen. She took it to the counter, where he guessed she'd pay and leave him to wonder about the desperation in her brown eyes.

But she didn't leave. She didn't pay. She set the paper on the counter near the cash register and began writing, the words streaming onto paper in large round letters.

Wes wasn't a snoop, but the words she wrote were so legible, and he was such a reader himself, that he wasn't able to resist taking a quick upside-down scan.

Sometime later I find myself . . .

She looked up into his eyes. Her right hand kept writing while she shrugged her straw handbag off her shoulder. It fell onto the counter.

. . . I find myself crawling onto . . .

She said, "Please take the money to pay for this out of my wallet."

. . . a grey . . .

He frowned. He knew better than to reach into a customer's handbag.

She said, "Please."

Those eyes. He found her wallet in her bag on top of a thick wad of computer paper covered with her round handwriting. When he opened the wallet, he read the name on the return-to-owner card inside.

Jamie Stewart.

He began to feel a little like a peeping Tom. He attempted to even up the score by offering his own name. "I'm Wes Gates."

She turned back a page and began writing again at the top. "My name's Jamie."

Wes took three dollars out of her wallet, rang up the sale, and slipped her wallet, with the change in it, back into her bag. All the while, she stood hunched over the counter. She reached the bottom of the page, turned it back, and began a new one.

She was a writer. That fit. He knew writers because they were thick on the ground in his family's circle of acquaintances. Without exception, writers were strange ducks. Most of them were likeable enough, although when it came to talking about their work, they were single-minded juggernauts.

Jamie wrote on like said juggernaut and didn't look up. She showed no sign of wanting to leave. A writer so focused might win a prize for creative concentration. Indeed, a woman this dedicated to the craft might indeed have won awards.

A teenager entered, paid for his chewing gum over Jamie's shoulder, and stared down at her paper curiously. He shrugged and left.

Wes watched Jamie work. He noted that she never crossed out or paused for thought. The roundly written words continued their swift progress down the yellow legal pad.

He wondered whether she'd published anything, or whether she was the type of aspiring obsessive who worked on her stories more than she talked about them. *Jamie Stewart.* Aside from the Hollywood connection, the name didn't sound familiar. It was easy to imagine *Jamie Stewart* printed on a book spine, though. He wondered what sort of writing she did. He was a thriller enthusiast and rather hoped she didn't write romance.

But that was none of his business. Not her genre or her romantic condition. Definitely not her third finger, bare where a wedding band would be.

Wes moved around Jamie and cleared the far end of the counter, moving candy and boxes of horoscope mini books onto an already crowded shelf on the other side of the register. He frowned at the powdered sugar and dust the display had hidden and gave the counter a wipe with his flannel sleeve.

With care he guided Jamie, still writing, a couple of feet over to the area he'd cleared for her. Once he had her settled there, he was not satisfied with his efforts. For one thing, he knew writers who wrote in cars, in bars, in bed, and even in the bath, but never standing hunched over a counter in a stranger's convenience shop. She was bound to get a headache in that position. Without further thought, he pulled his padded stool from behind the register and eased it underneath her.

She didn't look up, but he saw her smile behind her curtain of dark hair. Only for a moment, though, and then the smile was gone, and she was writing faster than before.

Wes stared. But not at the page. At Jamie. In case she smiled again.

The bell rang, and two customers entered the shop. The Ozalina sisters were regulars, older women who raised collies kindly if illegally in a house across the back lane from the shop. They came in daily, had done so since Wes was a small boy, always for dog food and often for air freshener.

Wes asked after the dogs and rang up the sale. As the women chattered about the most imminent litter, expected any hour, they shot glances at the silent young woman seated at the end of the counter.

The older of the Ozalina sisters finished her tale of bravery in the face of the law. "… and if the health inspector were not our niece, we would file for harassment. Who's that young person, Wes?"

Wes handed over their change. "She's a writer."

"Heavens." The Ozalina sisters exchanged glances and walked softly towards the door. "We won't disturb."

Wes thought that Jamie would hardly have noticed if the Ozalinas had climbed up on the counter to sing show tunes.

Jamie wrote on.

Chapter 5

Sometime later I find myself crawling onto a grey beach at the side of a slow-moving river. I lie stretched out and panting for breath. The sand under my cheek is moist and warm as flesh. I shudder, get to my feet, and look around.

Sand lies flat on the riverbank and continues outwards to a straight-edge horizon. The air is perfectly still. The river maintains a steady, silent progress past me, and I watch it until I get the feeling that it's watching me back.

I look down at myself. My body casts no shadow here, but at least I have a body, unlike at Dylan's house. It's really the only point in this geography's favour.

Because there's nothing else here. No plant life. No birds. No road. Only sky, sand, river, and direction.

I turn my attention back to the sky. To my left, past the river, white light glows from beneath the horizon. To my right lies the edge of night. I want neither pitch darkness nor the white light. Particularly not that. The only acceptable way is between the two, straight towards the grey horizon.

Forward or back? On principle, I step forward, but only on principle, because the two stretches of sand are identical in their lack of any feature. There's nothing else to do but walk straight on towards the grey horizon, with the slow-moving river to guide me. I don't want to think about the river, or the door, or the damp fleshy sand. I don't want to think about anything. I lift one foot and then the other. Swing my arms in opposition. Keep a little distance between me and the river. Eventually I become mentally grey, in tune with the sand and the sky.

After an unguessable length of time, I walk right through a streetlamp.

I'm not sure how I passed from the grey place to this residential street. Certainly, I wasn't paying attention, a bad habit I seem not to have cast off when leaving the living. So, some things you can take with you.

Overhead, the sun has nearly reached the roofs of the houses around me and turns the new growth on the mature trees golden. It's late afternoon. The house directly before me is one of the larger ones in view. It's dark brown with white trim, and overdue for a coat of paint. My mother would have had my father out long before this to touch up the trim of her house. To be honest, all the wives would have insisted upon it, and their mothers before them.

Even though it's still daytime, a light's burning in an open window on the top floor of the brown-and-white house, and I'm as certain as I can be that it's Dylan's light in Dylan's room. Don't ask me how I know the attic window is his, because this street is new to me.

I consider whether I should try to move straight up the side of the house. I can enter through the open window. Maybe it doesn't even have to be open.

Why not get some kicks? I could use a little fun. I tell myself that even though I'm dead, I'm young, and my grandfather always said that twenty was a feckless age. I want to be feckless. I want to be a lot of things I'm not—for instance, I'd like to be as visible here as I was on the beach and at the door. I'd like to move up the side of the house, scornful of physics. Then I'd sail in through the window and make Dylan jump.

But I'm a civilized person, so I enter Dylan's house through the front door. And *through* is exactly how I enter. I pass through solid wood as if it were a beaded curtain across a caravan door.

The entry hall at Dylan's house has a high ceiling, and above a broom's reach hangs a certain amount of spider webbing, appropriate for a haunted house. Because, now that I'm here, that's what it is. Except for the spiderwebs, somebody has taken great care to dust the place, and the entry's dark wood panelling and stair railings shine like the horse chestnuts I used to carry in my back pocket, throughout the autumn when I was in school.

On the foyer staircase a man and a woman sit side by side, both of them in dungarees and sweaters. The woman is old and the man less so, perhaps forty. Their faces crease in the same troubled lines, and the resemblance is obvious. This older one is the mother, and the younger is the son.

No. Move the decimal point up a generation. These are Dylan's father and grandmother.

I move across the foyer towards them.

They're speaking quietly together, her white head and his dark one bent close. I've been polite enough to enter through the door, but not polite enough to knock first. I decide to split the difference and leave them to speak privately.

But the father is talking about Dylan. "I can't do anything with that kid."

The grandmother's tone is impatient. "We have got to get him out of that room, Ethan. He's got to face facts. You heard the doctor. It might only be a matter of days. By the time he gets to the hospital …"

"It could be too late," Dylan's father finishes for her. "But, I repeat, I can't do anything with him."

I whisper, "Eureka," and dart up two flights of stairs to Dylan's room.

Now I know why I'm here.

I tear straight through Dylan's bedroom door and rise up, translucent but unmistakably myself, into the television light, right in front of his face. I might as well have said *boo*. He jumps a mile.

"Are you crazy? Don't sneak up on a person like that."

I go straight to the point. "Why didn't you tell me you're dying?"

Dylan turns down the volume of the television. "I'm not dying."

"Your father and grandmother were just talking about you on the stairs." A thought strikes me. "Have they kept the diagnosis from you? Didn't they tell you?"

"They tell me lots of stuff. Everybody tells me everything, they can't stop. One time somebody told me we're all dying as soon as we're born." He emits a dramatic groan.

I almost admire his nonchalance in the face of a sudden end to his brief existence. His life will be even shorter than my own, it's worth noting. Casual courage in the face of his mortality is all very well, but one of us had better step forward and take his illness seriously.

"This is life and death, Dylan. If you don't get to the hospital right away, it's only a matter of days."

"They're not talking about me. They're talking about my grandfather in hospital." Dylan sits back against the head of the bed and folds his arms.

I feel a wave of disappointment. I thought I had it all figured out. I'd make Dylan go to the hospital. I would save his life. And maybe after I saved him, I would move on and save somebody else. Like Rin Tin Tin in the movies, helping one person and then another. A hero, saving all in my path. This would be such an excellent reason for my ghostly condition that I have to tamp down my inappropriate displeasure with Dylan for not being sick.

I say, "Maybe you need to go see your grandfather in hospital. Maybe it would make a difference."

"It won't, and I won't."

"Explain, please."

"I keep telling everybody: I want to be part of his life here, at home where he belongs. I don't support his illness in any way. I reject it. I boycott it. And I don't want to discuss it, so don't say another word on the subject."

Dylan ought to visit the hospital every day. If it were my grandfather, I'd never leave his side.

I say, "I don't know how I died, but I would certainly have appreciated some visits from my family."

"I refuse to encourage him in being sick. And that's my final word on the subject." He narrows his eyes. "Anyway, why do you care so much about my grandfather?"

I can't help bursting, "At least your grandfather had a chance to get old. What about me? I didn't get more than a toe into my twenties."

"Wow," Dylan says. "How sensitive of you when I'm feeling bad about him."

"Sorry." I move out of the television light and gaze out the window. Night has fallen on Dylan's quiet neighbourhood. From up here, cars look smaller than they did in my day, but there are more of them. They move along the street with quiet hissing sounds, not with a rattle or roar. But the same triangular lights still nose along the blacktop ahead of them, like cow-catchers before a train. The moon will be up soon.

Dylan stands up on the bed, stares around the room, and collapses as if dropped from a height to lie face down on his pillow. I'm invisible in this corner of the room. The kid must think I've left again.

I open my mouth to reassure him but stop myself just in time.

Dylan's grandmother opens his door and walks into the room. She switches off the television set and stands with hands on hips, gazing down at Dylan. From her gentle mouth and straight carriage, I judge that she is both a loving elder and a tough cookie. She is obviously too smart to buy his possum act.

"It's way past time to go, Dylan. Visiting hours, remember?"

Dylan lies still.

"Don't think I believe you're asleep. You haven't been asleep before two in the morning for months. If I were your parent …"

She breaks off. A pause, a tsking sound, and she reaches down to stroke his hair.

"Dylan, if you don't get up off this bed, put on your coat, and sit your rear end down in the station wagon right now, I'm going to throw your television set out the window."

Dylan pushes her hand away. "You can't."

"I can." She flexes her arm and makes a muscle. "Seniors' weight training."

Dylan sits up at last. She hauls him to his feet and leads him out through the door, one arm around his stiff back. I hear them clearly on the stairs.

Dylan says, "I'll go, but I'm not getting out of the car."

"We'll see. I wasn't kidding about your TV."

"That's a seven-hundred-dollar set. And Grandpop gave it to me."

"That was his seven-hundred-dollar mistake. I'd give that television to the poor if they didn't have enough troubles."

They move out of earshot. I listen for the car to start up, but it's a long time coming. I stop caring. I don't want to move. A colourless quiet comes over me, reminiscent of my time at the grey riverbank. Within moments, my thoughts taper off. I stand like a piece of furniture by the window in the darkened attic room.

CHAPTER 6

"*Shh.*"

"No, you *shhh.*"

Hot breath brushed the crown of Jamie's head. She dropped her pen onto the legal pad and looked up from the pages of Casey's writing.

The convenience shop was much more colourful than her beige apartment, with shelves stacked with brilliantly labelled consumables and beach toys strung across the ceiling, but the two bright red heads of hair in front of her outshone everything in sight.

"Did we stop the flow?" one redheaded girl asked.

The second added, "Wes will kill us if we stopped your train of thought."

Neither girl appeared very worried.

Jamie remembered Wes, another redhead, perhaps an older brother to these two, just before she'd started writing Casey's story. Wes had helped her into this chair at the counter. "I don't think I thanked him. Has he left for the day?"

The first girl jerked her head towards the rear of the shop. "He's gone upstairs for supper."

"Are you hungry?" The second girl asked. Somewhere above them, dishes clattered. "You've been writing for hours."

"You're kind, but I should head home now." In fact, Jamie felt as empty as the beach buckets strung up over the cash register.

The first said, "She's starving. She's dying. Let's feed her."

"I'll carry your purse."

They pushed her through the doorway at the back of the shop and up a purple papered staircase. The two weren't identical, but they moved about so much and looked so much alike that Jamie was having trouble telling them apart. And now to cap matters, another redhead, the youngest yet, appeared on the landing at the top of the stairs. Behind her an arched doorway stood open. The curve at the top had been hand-lettered with the word *Experience*.

"Tiff, here is the Jamie Wes found in the shop."

"Gosh almighty," the one named Tiff said. "I'll tell Wes."

Jamie wondered at the welcome, and whether they might not have mistaken her for somebody famous or at least important. She ought to straighten them out on that, but she feared she'd drop first from hunger. She decided that she would eat something, thank them, and then explain that she was not a famous writer. Not a writer at all. Nobody, in fact.

The girls pointed at the quotation hand-painted above the archway. "That's Tennyson. *'All experience is an arch wherethrough gleams that untravelled world.'* It's a joke."

"It's not a joke." At the window of the over-furnished room, a woman rose from a sofa shaped like a clamshell, so gracefully that she might have been Botticelli's Venus rising from the sea. But of course this woman was wearing clothes. She pushed her long red hair back over her shoulders, walked forwards, and took Jamie's hand. "I'm Gloria Gates."

"She's our mother," Tiff said. "As if there were any doubt."

Great and grand, Gloria outmeasured Jamie by six inches.

"Here's Wes's writer, Jamie Stewart. Jamie, don't ask our mother about the quote by Tennyson."

Gloria's three daughters threw their hair back over their shoulders and hurried out of the room.

"Tennyson," Gloria Gates said, "must not be discounted, even at this late date. He was a Victorian, and nobody knows surfaces like the Victorians did. We're all children of the middle classes now, aren't we? Please sit down."

Jamie chose a sofa draped with patterned Indian cotton and fringe. There were enough of these plump sofas and big cushions jammed into the room to host a half-dozen reclining ancient Romans. At the windows, violet drapes were strung on wooden rods. Watercolours hung all about the room in small frames, like quilt squares.

Gloria Gates was still talking. Jamie had missed every word and begged her pardon.

"Not at all. I was saying that after the Victorians had fully explored life's surfaces, we had to wait more than half a century before Jim Morrison and the Doors would show us the inner mind of civilization."

Jamie had no reply to make, and silence was stretching into awkwardness when relief arrived in a tide of redheaded girls.

Tiff handed her a tray to balance on her lap. There was no dish or cutlery, but none was needed, for it was loaded with bread, cheese, and radishes with their green tops on. Washed, though.

The Gates women set trays on their knees, and Gloria gestured widely with her food in hand while expounding upon the theme of breaking through to the other side in Jim Morrison's lyrics and Tennyson's 'Ulysses'. Jamie got a thank-you in edgewise and began to eat.

Wes Gates walked into the room, bearing his own tray of food. He asked Jamie, "Better now?"

"Yes. This is very good cheese, Gloria."

Wes sat down on the sofa beside her.

Gloria said, "Jamie's a writer."

"We know that, Mom," he answered.

"We know that, *Gloria*," Gloria corrected.

"Gloria recently experienced a sizeable birthday," one of the middle girls said. "Having young people all around is rejuvenating only if none of us is calling her Mom."

"I don't know everybody's name," Jamie said apologetically.

"I'm Wes. You know that." He waved a radish at the nearest sister. "That's Riz."

"Her name is actually Horizon," Gloria said. "It's a lovely name. I don't know why you all have to shorten your names."

"The other one is Dove."

"Dove-of-Peace. Nicknames are a mockery," Gloria said.

"And Tiff."

"Tiff is short for Tiffany." Gloria sighed. "My salute to the eighties."

Tiff rolled her eyes at Jamie. "I'll bet you think that only Wes escaped the dreaded naming."

Gloria said, "His name is Western Sunset. Now, you're Jamie Stewart. You've done well to rise above your name. Both James Stuarts were kings who cared very little for the people they ruled."

"I was named for my father." Jamie often told this harmless lie, but the moment it left her lips, she regretted returning falsehood for kindness.

"However," Gloria continued, "*Al* Stewart was one of the more interesting musicians of the nineteen seventies. Dove-of-Peace, go and play 'Nostradamus' on the stereo, will you?"

Dove obliged. They ate from the trays on their laps, and 'Nostradamus' hummed under the talk like river sounds at a picnic.

Riz turned to her. "Do you give readings?"

"Of what? Oh." Jamie remembered that she was meant to be a writer.

Gloria said, "You are welcome to read from your latest project, if you like. We often host readings on Saturday evenings. You must stay. We've got a superb poet coming in tonight."

Dove-of-Peace made a rude face. "It's that Marly Blackstone, all dead fish and severed hands."

"Chaff and grain," her mother countered. "You've got to find the flashes of brilliance, diamonds in the dreck. He's not a bad poet, for a journalist."

Tiff, with the hard eyes of a crusader, interjected, "If you'd let us have TV, we'd get good at finding diamonds in the dreck."

"Expert, even," Riz agreed. "Discretionary to the max. What's your opinion, Jamie, as a writer? Does television kill the soul of a reader?"

Jamie did her best to rise to the conversational tone. "But do souls die? Isn't continuity traditionally the point of souls?"

"Good one, scribe." Wes grinned.

Jamie decided that it would be impossible even to begin explaining why she had written through a whole legal pad while not actually being a writer. She gave up on coming clean to these people, finished her cheese, and settled back into the corner of the sofa to listen. She might never be in a room like this again, so she'd be wise to enjoy it.

Riz continued, "At any rate, Blackstone can't be worse than that one last week. What was her name?"

Wes asked Jamie, "What's your comfort status? How about another cushion?"

"Better not." Jamie smiled. "I'm trying to stay awake. I don't want to miss anything."

"Last week's poet was named AVIC," Dove added. "I liked her."

"How could you, though? She was from a vegetable rights literary group," Tiff said, "and AVIC was an acronym for something."

"For what?"

Riz said, "I'll bet the *A* was for *atrocious.*"

Dove bridled. "She wasn't as bad as the performance artist who did disgusting things with yogurt."

"I cleaned that up," Gloria protested. "And we got a great turnout for him. We should get him back."

"What about that other free-verse woman, the one with the monkey?"

Tiff smiled. "I loved the monkey."

"She sold the monkey," Dove said. "She only likes marsupials now."

Jamie had not listened for the rough engine noise of the blue van once in the hours that she'd sat among the Gates family and their friends. A warm weight descended on her shoulders; Wes had tucked a gold-coloured afghan around her.

She felt safe from pursuit or harm in this warm room full of talk. Still, the feeling of safety was not safety itself. She had to leave. She had a forty-minute walk ahead of her, in the dark and alone.

Five more minutes before I never see them again, she promised herself. Just long enough to hear what lengths Gloria would go in defence of her poets.

When Jamie woke, she was half-buried in sofa cushions, the Gateses' living room teemed with strangers, and somebody was sitting on her feet. She pulled herself free and drifted in and out of sleep while Marly Blackstone declaimed poetry under the archway called *Experience.*

Sunday morning, Jamie came to with a jolt on the same sofa. She was not the only person sleeping over, for the poet Blackstone was snoring under the window. Sunlight moved across the Gateses' living room, and Jamie was content to lie still and watch it until the family stirred into action. Breakfast was a copy of supper the night before, with everybody eating with their fingers off trays on their laps. Jamie tried to help wash up, but Gloria said she was paying off a bet with her children — here she scowled at Blackstone — and help was not allowed. The three Gates girls rumbled down the steps to open the shop.

Jamie had Sunday off, and so did Wes. By this point she felt as if she'd known the Gates family for years, and she protested only faintly when he led her across the alley to the Ozalina sisters' place. There they spent the day grooming the half-dozen collie pups on hand until they gleamed with attention and care. Jamie was glowing too, although she was sure the warmth was inside her and invisible to the others. Her jeans and sweater were covered with dog hair. But when Wes asked, she said she would go to dinner at a Mexican café with him. He drove her to her apartment in his battered Le Mans to change her clothes.

"Dog hair suits you. Don't change for me." Wes apparently believed this to be a compliment. "But if you must, I'm happy to wait."

He pulled a paperback John D Macdonald out of the debris on the floor of the Le Mans's back seat, stretched his legs out across the front seat, and began to read.

Jamie ran upstairs to her apartment. She was pleased that Wes hadn't asked to come in. One look at her cold, boring rooms would give the show away. She wasn't the interesting person he seemed to take her for. Not a Gates kind of person at all.

She showered, brushed her hair, and pulled on a stretchy skirt and a sweater. They were a very quiet green, but at least they added colour to her face. She laughed aloud, for the colour recalled AVIC, the plant-rights poet. The acronym stood for *Against Vegetables in Cookery*. AVIC's first poem had been a three-page work comparing a vegetable garden with an abattoir, but Jamie recalled the second piece word for word.

Water boils,

a silent cry,

Too late!

Too soon!

Laughing, but with an eye on the clock, she took her flats out to the main room. She decided to buy some pictures to hang on the wall above the drab sofa. Riz and Dove had painted some of the watercolours that hung in the Gateses' front room. Perhaps if it wasn't too expensive, she might commission them to paint something. She would rather like a picture of a collie. Or perhaps a watercolour sketch of the archway with *Experience* lettered overtop.

Maybe both. Jamie stood so deeply plunged in thought, one shoe on and the other foot bare, that it was a moment before she became aware that one of her hands was off on its own again. She sat down on the sofa and put her hands under her thighs for safekeeping, but a moment later they pulled loose, and she watched her fingers move around atop the coffee table. The ghost was looking for paper again.

Jamie ran to the window, leaned over the sill, and called out to the Le Mans, "I can't come down, Wes. I'm sorry."

The car window on the near side was rolled up. Wes wouldn't hear her. Hopeless, even to think of descending. Furthermore, she sensed she had only a moment to find things to write on and write with. In a panic, she recalled to her the free blank notepads real-estate agents left in mailboxes. She'd stacked them in a drawer in the kitchen, along with several pens that must have come with the apartment, for they were all of them chewed at the top, and not by her.

She stumbled across the room to the sofa and dumped the notepads and pens across the coffee table. She selected one of each. Or the ghost did. She couldn't tell, and anyway, that was the least of her worries.

It took the last of her willpower to rise from the sofa and move to the window. If only Wes would roll down his car window, he might hear her shouted apology after all. She called, but got no answer. Seconds later, she was back on the sofa with her head bowed over an empty page.

Invisible and implacable, the ghost took her prisoner and marched her away.

CHAPTER 7

Fireworks explode in my face, and I wake in Dylan's room. I'm standing on the bench near the open window, and the moonlight pouring in feels as warm as summer sunshine. Dylan is standing in the shadows in front of me, grinning like a madman and snapping his fingers at what I recognize, after a moment of doubt, as a camera.

"Come on, come on," he growls at it.

I remember my brother Ted at the dials of our new radio, the top-notch one our father, after months of angling by my mother, bought in the spring of '36. It was shaped like a cathedral door, and Ted would kneel in front of it to tune in the hockey game. Top of the range it might have been, but it still took a few minutes to warm up. He'd mutter *Come on, come on.*

"Is there still hockey?" I ask Dylan.

He looks up sharply. "Quit making me jump like that."

I shrug. "I'm a ghost. I guess a little scaring is allowed, or even expected."

"Huh. Well, sure, there's hockey. We all watch the televised games, and Grandma cooks chilli." He returns to muttering at his camera. It buzzes back at him, and a moment later he waves a small photograph in the air like it's the banner of the winning team. "Got you."

"Don't you know anything about taking pictures? You have to take them in full light outdoors."

"That was some primitive photographic science you had back then. Wait a sec." He tilts the photo this way and that to study the image. "There was this haunted house TV show a while back, and they got a picture of one of you ghosts. A photo of your *ectoplasm*. Not the clearest image or anything, but I thought, why not give it a try? Hang on while I check the developer."

You might have asked before you took the photograph. But it's useless to preach manners to Dylan.

While he squints at the photo, I look down at my ectoplasmic hands. I can see them clearly, lit by moonlight. I'm visible, at least to myself and Dylan. The discovery makes me want to howl at the moon like a sentimental dog. Will I actually show up in a photograph? My hands and arms appear paler but somehow more human than they did in the beams from Dylan's electric lamp and television.

"Want to see?" Dylan turns the photo and holds it up in front of me. I reach for it, and he lets go, but the picture flips through my fingers to the floor. I swear I touched it before it fell. I felt something. It might be wishful thinking. But maybe there's something in it worth pursuing.

"Sorry." Dylan appears embarrassed at handing something solid to a ghost, like saying *see?* to a blind person. He bends down to pick up the photo, but I tell him to stop.

I say, "I want to try something."

I step down from the bench, stoop, and place my hand over the photo on the floor. My palm sinks partway into the floor-board, and I bury the photo in my hand so that the small square is completely contained, like a leaf in amber. It's not exactly a feeling, but I sense I'm carrying something with me.

I get to my feet, and the picture rises with my hand. I hold it out to Dylan and meet his gaze. I can see he's impressed.

I peer down at the photo. The picture is dark and fuzzy, but I make out my outline at the window. I look unreal, of course, or else superimposed, like when a photographer forgets to change the glass slide and a family portrait gets mixed in with a sailor and his bride.

"That's me," I marvel. "Well, what do you know?"

But Dylan isn't listening. He picks up a half-empty cola bottle from the floor beside his bed. Now, without permission or even warning, he shoves it against my midsection.

Before I can give him a piece of my mind, he steps back and puts his hands on his hips.

"Cool."

There's a cola bottle where my insides would be if I had any. I can tell it's not glass, more like rigid cellophane. Like me, the bottle is partly transparent. I move, and the liquid sloshes. Dylan's little experiment violates every rule of courtesy and respect.

"I can't believe you did that. Are you planning to use me as an icebox?" I rage. "What's next, a pound of bacon?"

But when it suits him, Dylan seems able to ignore distractions. Even the ire of a ghost. He narrows his eyes at me. "Do that hovering thing again."

"With pleasure, to get away from you."

I rise up off the floor. And I'm angry, so I go straight through the roof. Literally.

When I slip through the ceiling, I feel the slight push of the bottle against me, the way I perceived the solid door when

I passed through it downstairs. I expect to lose the cola bottle when I pass through the roof, and I sincerely hope it falls on Dylan's head. But it comes with me. Even inside me, it seems unthinkable that a bottle could pass through wood beams and tar shingles, but it does. I have no explanation for this phenomenon.

But I myself am a phenomenon. Let somebody explain me.

I float above the roof for a moment, soaking in the moonlight, just me, the photograph in my hand, and the cola bottle in my middle.

When I grow bored, I descend and move sideways to drop the bottle on Dylan, who has climbed onto his bed and turned on the TV. He grunts and sits up.

With care, I push the photograph down through the top of his bureau and release it inside a drawer. Probably among his socks.

I say, "Turn off the darned television. If a ghost was in my room, I wouldn't be glued to some entertainment show."

"You're still here?" Dylan switches it off. "Well, how the hell am I supposed to know? Sometimes you're gone for ages."

"Don't swear." I shiver, remembering the door. Don't think about the door. Any door.

"Where are you *now*? Can't you keep still for even a minute?"

I'm resting in a shadowy section of Dylan's room, outside the moonlight's range. I'm about to say so when his father opens the door and enters.

He gazes around the room and does a double take. Although there happens to be a ghost in here, I imagine he's simply surprised to find that Dylan's turned off the television. He sits on the edge of the bed.

"You didn't come into the hospital with us, and I thought you might like to know how your grandfather is doing. Do you want to talk about it?"

"Of course I don't."

In my unlit corner of the room, I frown. My father and I talked. He talked about his insurance company, and I talked about seeing the wide world someday. I always knew he wanted the best for me, and that he thought his business was the best. But he listened while I talked about my ambitions, all right, and would joke that I should pack him in my suitcase when at last I left for my writing life in foreign nations.

Dylan's father says, "I'm trying to understand. He's not only your grandfather, he's my dad. I don't want him to die."

Dylan says, "Obviously. And he's not going to."

"Well, you must admit that it's possible. At least someday." His father squeezes Dylan's shoulder, and Dylan scowls. "Maybe a visit from you will do him good."

"Grandpop can work hard to get well and come home. That will do him more good."

When his father leaves the room, Dylan closes his door.

I return to stand by the moonlit bench at the window, where Dylan can see me best.

He shoots me a phoney smile. "See, that's why you're here, Casey. My family is encouraging fears of death to hang over this house like a shroud, so naturally we'd attract ghosts."

"Like flies."

His gaze sharpens. "I can see stripes on your shirt now. And are you wearing blue jeans?"

"Dungarees. So what?" I have an idea. I climb up on the bench in front of the window. "Come here, Dylan."

He frowns. "Why?"

I make my voice lower. "Come, Dylan." I think I sound pretty ghostly.

"No, I don't think so." He glances behind him at the door.

It's satisfying to know that I can do this haunting business correctly if I want to. I might have a long career ahead of me.

I bring my fist down as hard as I can on the windowsill, but my hand passes into it, and I don't even raise dust. "Look, I posed for your photographic experiments, and now it's your turn to get over here. I want to try something."

He hesitates a moment longer.

"Be fair, Dylan."

He walks towards me at last. "You better not do anything scary. Don't forget I'm just a kid."

"Just nothing. Knock it off. And climb in."

"In what?"

"In ectoplasm."

Dylan blinks. "I'd never fit inside your ectoplasm."

"I'd like to think of it as my suit of ectoplasm. And I think it'll fit you."

"You're older, but I'm taller."

"No, I'm taller. You'd know that if you could see my feet properly."

Dylan grimaces. "I guess. But what if something happens?"

"Like what?"

"Like I die, and you step out and live."

I'm taken aback. "Impossible."

"That's rich, coming from you." He thinks for a moment. "You promise not to kill me and step out alive?"

I nod.

"Say it."

"I promise."

"I'm still not doing it." But he climbs up on the bench and steps into my space.

I crane to see our reflection on the far side of the room. "See? Like a suit of clothes."

Dylan makes a face at his reflection. He still looks like Dylan, standing on the bench at the window. I'm only a silver outline, like one of those photographic mistakes. Ectoplasm contains him like cellophane wrapping up a Shirley Temple doll.

Dylan says, "This is pretty strange. Your ectoplasm suit doesn't feel like anything to me."

"Me neither. It's like we're in different spaces."

"Different dimensions," he corrects me. "But I can hear you fine."

"Good."

"In fact, you're a little too loud. It's all weird."

I move my arm out to the side, and Dylan's arm moves with me.

He says, "Now, that's way past weird."

"Try to lower your arm."

He can't.

"Now, try to get out of the ectoplasm."

He swears again. He struggles but can't get out. I release his arm for a moment, the way I let go of the photograph. His arm pops out of the centre of my chest, and then I trap it again inside my own arm.

I'm not only taller than he is, I'm stronger.

I say, "See, I can move you with me like I did the cola bottle and the photograph. Through walls or anything."

"So what?" He thrashes harder to escape. "I'm not a cola bottle. I don't need you to move."

"That's true," I say. "But you do need me to fly."

We step through the window into the night sky.

"Quit yelling," I tell Dylan. "You'll distract my concentration."

It's a long way down. He quits.

We're floating above the roof of his house. I've stopped here because I want to see whether Dylan starts another ruckus. If he does, I'll put him back in his attic.

He breathes heavily and mutters words that would have had him spitting soap for a week if my grandfather caught him. I perceive a light breeze, and we rock a little as it passes, our single shadow—a shadow cast by him, I take it, not my own translucent self—swaying on the moonlit roof beneath us.

I say, "Where's your sense of adventure?"

He groans, "Back in the attic with my stomach."

"Take a deep breath. Tell me when you're ready."

A long pause follows. I gaze at the stars. They seem closer than I remember, but maybe I'm simply taking them in more attentively than I used to.

I hear a small voice say, *"Ready."*

"You sure?"

"I will if you will."

Up we go.

Our arms are stretched out wide, like my brother Ted when he was small, playing aeroplanes. In spite of myself, I let out a *"Vroom!"* We angle up into the night. The ground spreads out underneath us like a big grey counterpane, and as we rise, the windows of the houses where people sit up late are scattered bright lights, so that it seems as if we're sandwiched between stars above us and below.

It's a fine night for flying.

The wind feels cool and the moonlight liquid. We bob and arch like a dolphin in the sky. I feel currents of warm and cold, like rollers, waves of air as big as the backs of dinosaurs to slide down, one after another, and into the treetops.

If Dylan has his eyes closed, that's his loss.

I head up the dark and windy slope of the sky. "Let's go again."

"I will if you will," Dylan repeats.

I peer down through the darkness at the ground and the sleepy town. This time I imagine a toboggan run. It's long and broad with the whole world as a brake-stop. Dylan is hollering again, but I can't blame him. I'm yelling too.

This time I brake too late. We shoot through a house, the rooms slipping past like dividers in an egg carton, and when we stop, everything is cold and black and smells of garden soil turned over on a rainy day.

We're underground. Dylan's silent, but I can guess what he's thinking. *Buried alive.* Him, anyway.

Before he can start grousing, I pull us up out of the earth and onto the grass of his front yard. I stand aside. Dylan falls free. He scrambles to his feet, and his shadow shivers across the garden. My eye catches the pallid gleam of something under a bush. Perhaps another like me, but lower down. Maybe the ghost of a dog. This is a happy thought, and I imagine a faithful ghostly companion to enliven my days and nights. But when I look again, I see it's a forgotten gardening trowel that catches the light from the streetlamp outside Dylan's garden.

Above us, clouds are creeping up the rim of the sky. I shiver. When they reach the moon, I'll lose the light, and I won't be visible any longer.

Dylan gives himself a shake and grins widely. Now that our flight is over, he seems to be enjoying himself. But he's like that when he plays with his computer too: blank-faced while he plays, exultant when the game is over.

"What a ride that was." He beckons me to follow him out of the front yard. We look up and down the street at the houses and the streetlamps. A car prowls by, slows, and the driver stares at Dylan and me before speeding away.

Dylan says, "Look, what if we stay at ground level this time? Hold us a few inches above street level and really smoke it."

"Smoke it?"

"Yeah. How fast can you go? If we take the first turnoff to the right, we'll be on the highway. Nothing but a few trucks this time of night."

"You mean like in one of your computer games?" I give him an ironic look that he misses.

"But if we hit anything, we'll pass right through it. It's completely safe. Almost too safe!"

"Safe for you," I answer. "I'm certainly not in danger."

He bounces on the balls of his feet, fists deep in his pants pockets. I look down at my jersey with its blue and red stripes. I wonder how Dylan can bear to wear black all the time. Black trousers black shirt black socks black shoes. I try to laugh at the thought, but unaccountably my mood has altered.

"Speeding around is a stupid idea," I say. "I wish I never took you flying."

"Come on, Casey. It'll be fun."

Fun?

All this ghost business—walking through walls, soaring up into the air—should be a lark. It should thrill me from my transparent head to my invisible toes. I've got magic powers: invisibility and seven-league boots. I should feel like a hero. A king of the world.

But in stories, magic powers get the hero something. The girl. A fortune. The life I've always wanted, seeing the world. Being the man I want to be.

But I'm past all that. I'm dead. There's no happy ending for me.

I try to envision a brilliant outcome for myself, but all I can think of is coming back to life. How can I achieve a goal like that? Not by using the power of invisibility. Not with seven-league boots.

"I don't want to tear around anymore, Dylan."

"What's the matter?" He peers at me. "You don't look so good."

In spite of everything, I have to laugh at the thought of a ghost not looking so good.

But out of the corner of my eye, I catch sight of something moving swiftly down the road towards us. It's moving too quickly to be a car. I reach for Dylan's shoulder, but of course my hand passes through him.

He tenses. "What is that?"

I can't make out its precise shape. All I know is that it's a vaguely vertical shape, and its path is towards us.

He says, "That light looks like the same kind of light that you are."

The light grows brighter still. Dylan is shivering now. But why? I'm a ghost, and he's not afraid of me.

There's even less reason for me to be afraid. Might this be another like me? Another ghost? Whose? It might be a friend from the old days. Or a long-gone relation.

This may be at last somebody who can tell me why I died so young, and why I've been gone from the world for half a century.

But equally it might be a terror, a walking curse of a corpse like some ghosts are said to be, rotting flesh hanging from blackened bones. A nightmare to track me along my eternity.

It's coming closer. Growing larger. Nearing Dylan and me.

I turn to Dylan. "Run."

He says through his teeth, "I'm not leaving you."

The light moves closer, faster.

Dylan points. "It's not just one thing. See? It's a group."

He's right. The light steadies as it nears us, and I make out in the distance five shapes slipping along the street.

Dylan says, "There's even a small one, there, right at the end."

The shapes don't look like people. These are not ghosts. Not like me, anyway.

They're half a block away.

Now they grow larger. No. They don't exactly grow.

They rise. The five are like branches of a tree with a thick trunk, swelling up out of the pavement. At last I make sense of the shape. I recognize it. I know what's rising out of the road to loom above us now, as high as the houses around us.

It's a hand. The palm stretches and descends, cupping as if to catch flies.

Again, I say, "Run," and this time he does. He's gone in a blink. And that's good, although by now I'm nearly certain that the hand doesn't want him.

I can't move. I'm pinned to the sidewalk. The hand is so large now that it blots out the sky. And just before it takes me, I see the stripes. The blue and red stripes on the jersey wrapped around its enormous wrist.

Whatever this is, it has taken the shape of my own hand.

It closes around me. Now the world is gone, and I'm crushed against the great palm, crumpled in on myself like a paper box. The hand moves, shakes me, as if testing me for weight. It tosses me aside.

I tumble head over heels and land, feet out, with my back up against something hard. I don't want to open my eyes. I open them.

I'm sitting up at the base of the door.

Something on the other side is working hard to push it open.

I shout my refusal. I dig my heels against the solid surface underneath me and shove my full weight against a growing pressure. My back holds the door that little bit ajar and will hold forever if necessary. I swear it.

Chapter 8

Wes Gates could no longer disregard the length of time he'd been waiting for Jamie to return to the Le Mans so he could take her out to dinner.

The sun was declining. He stuck his thumb between the pages of the paperback he'd been reading and looked up through the passenger window at Jamie's apartment building. The front door was shut, and through the foyer window he could make out no movement inside. He'd already read *The Quick Red Fox* more times than most people would believe, which was ironic, because he'd been waiting here for Jamie longer than most fellows would sit around for.

In fairness it could be argued, maybe even should be argued, that sitting around was Wes's chosen profession, given his daily grind of ringing up purchases on the family cash register at their convenience store. He appreciated that his job equipped him with patience, but, like a police officer who carries a gun on the job, he didn't want to have to use it in his personal life.

He considered honking to let Jamie know he was still here and getting tired of waiting, but instantly dismissed the thought as crass and, in fact, unworthy of new nineties principles of mutual respect between genders. Then he reconsidered, thinking of the new nineties openness of communication. *If you want to honk, go for the gold.* But for Wes, the philosophy of courtesy he'd developed in the shop and his mother's salon was as solid as the earth beneath his feet. He would maintain his manners no matter the odours of discord around him.

For example, honking at a person such as Jamie, who kept a guy waiting in a car for extended periods of time, would be discourteous. But a guy didn't want to treat himself poorly either, for example being a patient doormat. He tried, as an exercise in comparative behaviourism, to imagine waiting this long for any other person of his acquaintance. He created a ratio comparing the irritation of waiting with the loveliness of the person awaited; but in the end the ratio was irrelevant. Courtesy couldn't exist if it required reciprocation. Courtesy acted of itself. So he'd wait, and he wouldn't honk.

Then he did honk, as a warning, because a blue van pulled up behind him, so close that its nose nearly touched the rear of the Le Mans. A moment later, the passenger doors swung open to let out a man and a woman. Because of the sort of useless trivia his mind collected in its lintier corners, he observed that the woman was older and the man younger, and the woman had been driving.

The pair approached Wes's car.

The man said, "Sorry about that. I swear she didn't touch you."

Wes rolled down the driver's window. "And I'm sorry about the honk. I'm sure everything was under control."

The woman wore approximately half a smile. "You don't like women drivers?"

"I have no opinion on drivers anywhere, of any description."

"You for a quiet life," the man said. "Say, do you know this area?"

"No." Wes almost added, *I'm waiting for a friend*, but once he'd said that to a journalist his mom knew, and the journalist had snapped back, *Can't she do her own waiting?* So he said, "I'm awaiting a friend."

The man said, "Sure. Some individuals are worth waiting for, right?"

Wes noted that it was possible for people to be both obnoxious and correct.

The woman said, "We're looking for particular apartment building numbers. Can you read that one?"

Wes could. "Looks like 2974."

The man nodded. "The system is working."

"We should have brought a map," the woman said.

Wes had a map of the city folded up in his glove compartment, but when he offered them its use, the man shook his head. "We've got a system. We'll hit building 2972, then 2974. Let's go."

"Don't forget your clipboard," the woman said.

Her companion winked humorously at Wes, revealing himself to be not only unlikeable but unobservant of the new decade's mores, and the two retrieved their clipboards from the van dash. They hurried off towards the apartment building next to Jamie's, leaving the van apparently unlocked. For a swift retreat? Wes laughed to himself. He almost wished he'd asked them what they were looking for, but he'd had enough of that pair. In the convenience store game, you were friendly with all customers and selective about the length of time you spent with them. The two with their blue van weren't by any means charming people, but they seemed harmless.

The fellow was right about one thing. Some people were indeed worth waiting for, but the statement's correlation reminded him that some had no wish to be awaited. If this was Jamie's version of the brush-off, it was working, but how to know if it was? It might equally be a test of his interest, but that would be romantic gamesmanship of the sort practised mainly in the Middle Ages and involving jousts and boar hunts. But if this were not the brush-off, he should ask more deeply about her writing career. Balance interest with nosiness. Pushiness with doormat-ism.

Wes shook his head. Everything was easier when you were goofing around with collie dogs.

The clipboard-carrying pair had now entered the apartment building next to Jamie's, number 2972. Their swift progress stirred Wes to take action of some kind. Then again, they weren't really the sort of people a guy would want to emulate. *Be cool.*

Wes opened his book. He'd give her one more chapter. Then he'd go up and find her.

§

In Pulp Literature *Issue 44, Autumn 2024, look for 'Exit Light, Enter Night,' Part 3 of* Take My Hand: A Ghost Story, *as Casey's determination and power grows, and Jamie's danger deepens.*

THE ARTISTS

Joyce Harumi Kamikura
Cover artist, Yellow Moon

Born in Steveston, British Columbia, Joyce spent the first four years of her life in the internment camp at Lemon Creek. She then lived in Japan for nine years, after which she returned to Canada, lived in Montreal for two years, and eventually returned to Richmond, BC. After earning her Bachelor of Commerce and Business Administration degree from UBC, Joyce studied art at both Kwantlen and Langara colleges.

In 1993, Joyce had the honour of being recognized as a Signature Member of the National Watercolor Society (NWS-USA), making her one of the first Canadians to receive this distinction. In the same year, she achieved the prestigious title of Senior Signature Member (SFCA) with the Federation of Canadian Artists, being among the first women to attain this top-ranking position as awarded by her peers.

Joyce's paintings represent her world as seen through her artistic eyes. Her ideas are fragments of what fascinates and intrigues her, and are the roots from which the works begin to emerge. A habitation on the mountain by Deer Lake in Burnaby was just such an inspiration that whistled at Joyce, transforming what she saw into shapes, colours, and lines. It became an excuse for her to paint, exploring possibilities and permutations, removing a good deal from reality. To see more of her work, visit joycekamikura.ca.

Michaela Chan
Creator, 'Fasteners'
Michaela Chan is a book artist who writes and illustrates stories that explore the comforts of uncertainty. Her narratives have been published in *The Rumpus, The Offing, The American Medical Association Journal of Ethics*, and elsewhere. Before she graduated with a degree in biochemistry, questions of race prompted Chan's scholarship-sponsored study of American race relations. She wanted to know if she was white. At the School of the Art Institute of Chicago, Chan completed graduate work in writing with a concentration in graphic narrative and book arts. Currently an artist-in-residence at Flower City Arts Center in Rochester, New York, Chan teaches bookbinding and develops new stories. See more of her work at michaelachan.com.

Mel Anastasiou, *in-house illustrator*
Mel Anastasiou loves drawing for *Pulp Literature* because she loves the stories she illustrates. She draws in black and white, working from imagination and inspired by details from Renaissance compositions. You can find illustrations, writing tips, and news about her books and novellas at melanastasiou. wordpress. com, and see more of her artwork on Face-book at Bird and Branch Artwork.

HALL OF FAME

These are the heroes — the Patrons and Pulp Literati whose monthly support helped bring you this issue. Please lift your glasses and give them a rousing cheer!

The Brewers
Dana Tye Rally

The Innkeepers
Andrea Kepple
David Jensen
Ev Bishop
Gillian Gardiner
Kevin Harris
Lorna Ens
Mark Francis
Richard Ohnemus
Robin McGillveray
Susan Jackson

The Cicerones
Jennifer Sommersby
Roger & Anne Anastasiou

The Bartenders
Alana Krider
Andrea Kirkham
Anna Belkine
April DC
Benjamin Johnson
Bjarne Hansen
Brighton Hugg
Bryan Moose

Chris Olee
Dave Wayne
Deepthi Atukorala
Ernst Pulido
Finnian Burnett
Fran Scannell
James Carlino
Jennifer Getsinger
Jillian Shoichet
John Olley
K Anastasiou
Katherine Derbyshire
Katriona Greenmoor
kc dyer
KT Wagner
Leny Wagner
Lin & John Richardson
Margaret Elliott
Margot Landels
Margot Spronk
Maureen Cooke
Megan Shaw
Michelle Balfour
Mike Sylvester
Peter Halasz
Rapscallion
Richard Gropp
Ron Graves

Scott F Gray
Scott Carrothers
Shannon Saunders
Star
Suzanne Philip
Venasa Simpson
Devan Erno

The Regulars
Adam Fout
Akemi Art
Andy W
BC
Catherine Levinson
Charity Tahmaseb
David Perlmutter
James Gotaas
Jenny Blackford
Marilyn Holt
Marta Salek
Meredith Frazier
Paul Anguiaro
Rhea Rose
Rina Piccolo
Sonia Brock
Vera
Emmy Bee
JS Andrew

If you would like to join the ranks of these worthies, you can become a patron on Patreon at patreon.com/pulplit or join the Pulp Literati through our website at pulpliterature.com/join-pulp-literati/.

IGNITE YOUR IMAGINATION

30 yrs of award-winning sci-fi and fantasy

WWW.ONSPEC.CA

In search of a writing community?

Join today!

The Federation of BC Writers is here for you!

- ☑ Workshops/ Webinars
- ☑ Contests
- ☑ Readings
- ☑ Articles

- ☑ Networking
- ☑ Discount Membership for for Students and Seniors

- ☑ Digital Writing Circles
- ☑ Find Inspiration & more!

bcwriters.ca/Join

Keep it weird.
Subscribe today!

GEIST
FACT + FICTION • NORTH of AMERICA

THE LOWEST TIDE
My Summer Behind the Iron Curtain
Everything As It Was / On Lake Saiko
Erasure Contest Winners / Main Character

GEIST
go to geist.com/subscribe
or call 1-888-GEIST-EH

FACT + FICTION • NORTH of AMERICA

MARKETPLACE

Books

Advent *by Michael Kamakana* • We thought we knew what the aliens wanted. Think again. • pulpliterature.com/advent

Allaigna's Song: Chorale *by JM Landels* The long-awaited conclusion to the bestselling *Allaigna's Song* trilogy. • pulpliterature.com/allaignas-song

The Extra: A Monument Studios Mystery *by Mel Anastasiou* • Extra Frankie Ray gets her big break on the Silver Screen, until murder steals the scene. • pulpliterature. com/the-extra

The Labours of Mrs Stella Ryman: Further Fairmount Mysteries *by Mel Anastasiou* • Trapped in a down-at-the-heels care home. You'd be cranky too. • pulpliterature.com/stella-ryman-and-the-fairmount-manor-mysteries

What the Wind Brings *by Matthew Hughes* • Winner of the 2020 Endeavour Award • pulpliterature.com/product-category/novels/matthew-hughes

The Writer's Boon Companion *by Mel Anastasiou* • Thirty Days Towards an Extraordinary Volume • pulpliterature.com/subscribe/the-bookstore

Bookstores

Russell Books • 100-747 Fort St, Victoria, BC • russellbooks.com

Western Sky Books • 2132-2850 Shaughnessy St, Port Coquitlam, BC V3C 6K5 • 604-461-5602 • store.westernskybooks.com

White Dwarf / Dead Write Books • 3715 10th Ave W, Vancouver, BC V6R 2G5 • 604-228-8223 • whitedwarf@deadwrite.com

Conferences & Events

When Words Collide • August 10-12, 2024 Calgary, AB • whenwordscollide.org

Wine Country Writers' Festival • 27-29 September, 2024 winecountrywriters-festival.ca

Surrey International Writers' Conference October 2024 • siwc.ca

Printing & Publishing

First Choice Books/Victoria Bindery Book printing & binding • graphic design • eBooks • marketing materials 1-800-957-0561 • firstchoicebooks.ca

Writing Resources

Dreamers Creative Writing • Workshops, residencies, contests & more! • www.dreamerswriting.com

Magazines

Amazing Stories · Back in print! amazingstories.com

Arc Poetry Magazine · Poetry, essays, interviews, reviews · arcpoetry.ca

The Digest Enthusiast · Digests past & present plus new genre fiction larquepress.com

EVENT Magazine · Poetry & prose eventmagazine.ca

Geist · Ideas + Culture · Made in Canada · geist.com

Malahat Review · Poetry, fiction, creative non-fiction · www.mysteryweekly.com

Mystery Weekly Magazine · The cutting edge of short mystery fiction www.mysteryweekly.com

Neo-opsis · Canadian magazine of science fiction based in Victoria, BC · neo-opsis.ca

OnSpec · The Canadian magazine of the fantastic · onspecmag.wordpress.com

Polar Borealis · Paying market for new Canadian SF&F writers & artists · polarborealis.ca

Room Magazine · Literature, Art & Feminism since 1975 · roommagazine.com

The Malahat Review

ESSENTIAL POETRY • FICTION • CREATIVE NONFICTION

Open Season Awards

$6000 prize money in three categories

- poetry
- short fiction
- creative nonfiction

Commit these deadlines to memory

February 1, 2025
Long Poem Prize | $2500
Two writers split the winnings

May 1, 2025
Far Horizons Award for Short Fiction | $1250
One writer gets the prize

August 1, 2025
Constance Rooke
Creative Nonfiction Prize | $1250
One winner takes all

University of Victoria

malahatreview.ca
malahat@uvic.ca

THE MAGICAL CONCLUSION TO THE MUST-READ EPIC TRILOGY

the adventures of Allaigna sing

simply a joy to read

keeps you turning pages from beginning to end

an immensely satisfying epic

CONTESTS

Pulp Literature runs six annual contests for poetry, flash fiction, short stories, and novel first pages. For contest guidelines, prizes, and entry fees, see pulpliterature.com/contests.

The First Page Cage
Contest opens: 1 August 2024
Deadline: 15 September 2024
Winner notified: 15 October 2024
Quarter-finalists published online: Autumn 2025
Prize: $300

The Raven Short Story Contest
Contest opens: 1 September 2024
Deadline: 15 October 2024
Winner notified: 15 November 2024
Winner published: Issue 46, Spring 2025
Prize: $300

The Kingfisher Poetry Prize
Contest opens: 1 October 2024
Deadline: 15 November 2024
Winner notified: 15 December 2024
Winner published: Issue 46, Spring 2025
Prize: $300

The Bumblebee Flash Fiction Contest
Contest opens: 1 January 2025
Deadline: 15 February 2025
Winner notified: 15 March 2025
Winner published: Issue 47, Summer 2025
Prize: $300

The Magpie Award for Poetry
Contest opens: 1 March 2025
Deadline: 15 April 2025
Winner notified: 15 May 2025
Winner published: Issue 48, Autumn 2025
Prize: $500

The Hummingbird Flash Fiction Prize
Contest opens: 1 May 2025
Deadline: 15 June 2025
Winner notified: 15 July 2025
Winner published: Issue 49, Winter 2025
Prize: $300

EVENT

36th ANNUAL NON-FICTION CONTEST

INCREASED CASH PRIZES
$1,500 • $1,000 • $500

OCTOBER 15

Non-Fiction Contest winners feature in every volume since 1989 and have received recognition from the Canadian Magazine Awards, National Magazine Awards and Best Canadian Essays. All entries considered for publication. Entry fee of $34.95 includes a one-year subscription. We encourage writers from diverse backgrounds and experience levels to submit their work.

eventmagazine.ca

FIND FANTASTIC NEW WORLDS THIS SUMMER!
Subscribe to Pulp Literature and be swept away!
pulpliterature.com/subscribe
PULP Literature
Kelly Robson
'La Vitesse'
CC Humphreys
Graham J Darling
Mel Anastasiou
Jordan Bray
Cat Girczyc
JM Landels
Robert J Sawyer
'Above It All'
Mel Anastasiou
Franco Amati
Sierra Louie
JM Landels
EC Dorgan
JJ Lee
Finnian Burnett
'When Captain Picard Was My Dad'
Good books for the price of a beer!
JM Landels
Preston Lang
Nat Kishchuk
Mel Anastasiou
Wiley Wei-Chiun Ho
Good books for the price of a beer!
NEO-OPSIS 
Science Fiction Magazine
www.neo-opsis.ca

Become a Patron of Pulp Literature

By supporting *Pulp Literature* on Patreon with $2 or more per month, you will be laying the foundation for a secure future for the magazine, as well as ensuring that you never miss an issue! Your subscription includes four big issues of short stories, novellas, poetry, comics, and novel excerpts, delivered to your door or electronic mailbox each year. **Find us at patreon.com/pulplit**

If you prefer to subscribe through our website, go to pulpliterature.com/subscribe.

Or you can send a cheque with the form below to
Subscriptions, Pulp Literature Press, 21955 16 Ave, Langley BC, V2Z 1K5, Canada

---

Don't miss an issue!

❏ **Send me 2 years (8 issues) at the special rate of $110** (save $34)*
❏ **Send me 1 year (4 issues) for $60** (save $12)*
❏ **Send me 2 years of digital issues for $35** (save $12.92)
❏ **Send me 1 year of digital issues for $20** (save $3.96)

Name: ____

Address: ____

City: ____ Prov. / State: ___________

Postal code: ________________ Country:______________________________

Email: ____

❏ Payment enclosed
❏ Bill me
❏ New
❏ Renewal

Make cheques payable in Canadian funds to Pulp Literature Press. Include email address for digital editions and Paypal billing, or subscribe at www.pulpliterature.com/subscribe.

*for postage outside Canada add $20 per year in North America or $32 per year overseas.